# THUGGA

*A novel by B.R.*

Support Our Black Authors Publishing INC.

P.O. Box 690360

Bronx, N.Y. 10469

D0067415

ISBN 978-0-578-08368-1

www.brthewriter.com

email BR@BRTHEWRITER.COM

Twitter: Twitter.com/@brthewriter

THUGGA

# Dedications

This book is dedicated to my mom. That was a hell of a fight, I'm sorry I couldn't be there to help and see you through. You're stronger than I am. I would have given up a long time ago...I love you. To my sisters Jada and Simone, my niece Anaya, my cousins Elijah, Damiso, Josiah, Rodney, Triffy, Jason, Cristina, Jermaine, Sean, Lenox, Toya, that crab ass Kevin even though you turned your back on me when I needed you the most, my brother in law Steven, and Aunty Claudette. To Joe, Tiffany and Bronx National, thanks for putting me in all them hot whips. I'm going to buy my first Bentley from you guys. To Nadjah Allen, thank you for helping me discover Arizona. I love it there and that's where I plan to spend the rest of my life. Shaunna Saloman, I see you on your actress shit do your thing baby girl. To my grandparents Lucille and Keith Henry, my god, where would I be without you guys. I would have went crazy if you two aint hit that visit floor every weekend. Grandpa Pee-Wee, my aunt Pam, Angie, Fay, and Uncle Al, may god bless ya'll. To Vickie Cumberbatch—wow, if people only knew our story. I think we had to have been the craziest couple alive, what a ride that was. To Angela, Su Gottie (aka) 5, Pop, J-Savage (aka) Hova, Shine, Bleek, Ghetto, Thugga, thanks for letting me use your name and making it a hot book. R.I.P. my dad Glenn Roy Hines, Uncle Robby, my big Homie Puke, I miss you all. Buck what's poppin kid!!! It's me and you to the end homie. My cousin Gary, sorry I left you with that bill, I got you tho kid. Aunt Janet and Uncle Paul, Nika, Paul JR. were you at Kid? Terry-Ann, whaagwan bredren? To the birth place of my mom and dad, Jamaica stand up. Bronx, Staten Island, Brooklyn, Harlem, Queens, stand up New York is definitely in the building. To Daniel—wow, who ever knew, if he ever knew, lol. To my Support Our Black Authors Publishing family, it's been hard but trust me, it will get harder. We gotta start small, but trust me, at the end we'll be on top. My homies Poppy, Grav, Mack 11, hold your head scrap, Pistol, damn homie I wish it aint happen that way for you but keep the faith, appeals is a mother fucker. K.T., J-money (aka) Jim Ice R.I.P. 730, Jah Long, Uncle-O where you at kid? Drip (NINO, 241), Bronx Tale, Copito, my lil' ma Nikki [AKA] Big Booty Judy. Thank you all, you all played a special part in my life, love you all.

Special Thanks to my editor Damiso. I know I gave you hell; my spelling is the worst, thanks for all the help kid. To get in contact with Damiso for editing work email him at d.hutchinson24@hotmail.com.

Another special thanks to the man who started this all, Gahsh of omyGahsh productions. Thanks for saving me from these niggas, they couldn't make book covers to save they life. You a bad dude, talented like no other. I can't wait to see what you do with the other book covers. You can reach Gahsh at www.omygahshproduction.com. He also does movies, music, pictures, websites and more.

Last but not least, to my little cousin Jeremih who was born today, Tuesday April 5th. We got you lil homie. Never will you need for anything, break bones of whoever touch you. Your dad (Jason Sylvester) Uncle Rod and I got you. Don't worry about nothing.

# Chapter 1

*Tiffany*

"Good morning Mr. Baker" Tiffany said looking up from her desk as he walked in late for work. "A little late this morning aren't we?"

"Yes, I apologize Tiffany the traffic from Brooklyn to the Bronx was absolutely ridiculous this morning, plus the rain didn't help either. Did I receive any phone calls?"

"No sir but we have a problem."

"Who is it this time?"

"Mrs. Taylor, she's late with her payment again."

"That's three months in a row. I'll take care of it."

The middle aged five foot three man was losing his hair and the car insurance business was gonna help him loose his mind. Tiffany was only a secretary; it was his responsibility to call the clients that paid late. Mr. Baker walked pass Tiffany and into his office.

"Tiffany, please bring me the folders of the new clients we got yesterday."

The folders were sitting on Tiffany's desk. Mr. Baker could have grabbed them himself but he enjoyed seeing the body of his beautiful young secretary, and Tiffany knew it; it became a routine. He would come in every morning walk by her then ask for something to be brought into his office—that way he could admire her figure without being noticed, at least that's what he thought.

Tiffany walked in his office with a white business shirt on, black heels, and a grey skirt that showed off her sexy smooth long legs, with an ass so perfect she could be an apple bottom model. Small waist, flat stomach, with just a hint of a six pack, breast just enough for a mouthful with the face of an angel and a Halle Berry hair cut. Tiffany's 21 years old. Insurance was not what she wanted to do with her life but it pays the bills. Insurance secretary by day, college student by night where she was studying to become a nurse and nothing was gonna stop her.

"Here you go Mr. Baker."

Tiffany handed him the folders and started to walk back to her desk as Mr. Baker swallowed hard and loosened his tie, 'my God look at that ass' he thought to himself watching her sway it back and forth as she walked.

8

"Mr. Baker, will there be anything else?" Tiffany asked stopping suddenly and turning around on purpose catching Mr. Baker watching her.

"Oh, uhm, no Ms. Jones, that will be all."

"OK." She smiled to herself at the surprise look on his face as she caught him staring. She returned to her desk in time to catch the phone as it rang.

"Hello, Baker's insurance, this is Ms. Jones speaking, how may I help you?"

"Tiffany it's me, your mother."

"Oh, hey ma. I hope this is important Mr. Baker just walked in" Tiffany whispered.

"Damn girl now your mother gotta have something important to talk about just to call you?"

"Mom you know I didn't mean it like that—are you ok?"

"Yeah I'm ok, just wondering why my only child didn't call her mother last night."

"I'm sorry mother I got in late last night from school. Midterms are coming up and I stayed at the library to study."

"Tiffany you need a good man, like this guy I met this morning."

"Please stop trying to hook me up mom."

"But Tiffany, he's so nice and cute."

"Ms. Jones can I see you for a minute please?"

"Mom I have to go—bye."

Tiffany hung up the phone shaking her head. Her mother was always trying to hook her up on blind dates. Tiffany felt she didn't need anyone—ever since Jermaine died that is. Jermaine was her last boyfriend. She loved him and was going to spend the rest of her life with him, until one day she got a phone call. He had been hit by a drunken driver as he was crossing the street on his way home from work. Jermaine died instantly, without Tiffany having a chance to tell him goodbye; no last touch, no last kiss. That was two years ago and she has been single ever since.

"Yes Mr. Baker?"

"These files right here are complete."

"Okay I'll give them all a call and ask them to come in and sign."

"Thank you."

As Tiffany walked away she was pretty sure Mr. Baker was watching. He didn't make her feel uncomfortable, but more like wanted. She knew the old man would never get some. She sat at her desk, opened the folders, and made the call to the first client.

"Hello?"

"Hello Ms. Trinity my name is Ms. Jones from Baker's insurance."

"—yes, and?"

"Your insurance is ready and we were wondering if you can come in today for signing."

"*No I cannot.* You people always want someone to drop what they're doing because you're ready, I'll be in tomorrow" the lady said hanging up the phone. Tiffany had to laugh.

"Some people are too much", she opened the other folder 'Mr. Sean Clark' she said to herself as she dialed his number.

"Yo what up...who dis?"

A voice so deep and sexy came through the phone it sent chills through Tiffany's body.

"Oh, Mr. Clark my name is Tiffany Jones from Bakers Insurance, your file has been completed

11

and we would like for you to come in and sign at your earliest convenience."

"Aight, and you can call me Sean you dig sweetheart."

"Okay, Sean" Tiffany answered now blushing; his voice was driving her crazy. Tiffany wiggled in her seat, her clit was throbbing, it's been a long time and she was trying to gain control.

"Will that be today Sean?"

"Nah, more like tomorrow, anywhere from 12 to 2, we good with that?"

"Yes, yeah, sure Sean that will be great."

"Oh yeah and Tiffany"

"Yes?"

"I can't wait to meet you, you sound sexy as shit."

Before Tiffany could say anything he hung up. In a way she couldn't wait to see him either.

# Chapter 2

*Thugga and Kiki*

"Damn Thugga you just gonna play me like that? Right in front of my face you gonna tell a bitch you can't wait to meet her and I'm bout to give you some pussy?"

"Come on Kiki you know I ain't mean that shit, that's the insurance chick, just having some fun that's all; bitch probably fat, old and ugly" Thugga said calming her down.

Thugga sits his blackberry down on the hotel table as he turned around and looked at Kiki's naked body, her golden brown skin looking ever so soft. Thugga's dick got hard instantly, as he got naked he stood there looking at Kiki's hairy pussy, as it started to get wet she put her fingers on her clit and started playing with it, her clit was throbbing and pussy ready to be fucked.

"Come on daddy don't make me beg, don't make me wait", Kiki used her free hand to grab her breast and play with her nipples.

Thugga grabbed her by her ankles and pulled her to the edge of the bed and slobbed her down. By this time his dick was hard as a rock.

"Go head daddy give me one of them good fucks I love so much."

Thugga slid all nine inches of his dick in her wet warm pussy. She grabbed hold of his back as she took his dick.

"Ahhhh! Yes daddy, get it."

Thugga pumped his dick in and out of Kiki's fat, wet, soft pussy.

"Put your legs on my shoulders bitch."

Kiki didn't miss a beat as she put her legs up on his shoulders; it gave Thugga the room to get his dick deeper into her.

"Ahhh! Yeah daddy you feel so fucking good."

Kiki started to get wetter than before. You could hear her juices whenever he went in and out of her.

"Turn the fuck around."

Kiki did as she was told with no problem. Thugga ate her out from the back, his tongue going up and down on her clit sucking up all her juices as it dripped down her pussy. He got up smacked her on her ass with his dick and watched her soft ass shake. He rammed his dick into her pussy again; Kiki took it like a pro, loved it and wanted more. Thugga kept on pumping and smacking Kiki's fat ass with every pump. Kiki would yell out, "more, more", it turned him on so much.

"I'm gonna cum!" as soon as he said that Kiki turned around grabbed his dick and started to suck on his head; as he came in her mouth he yelled "ughhh!" stepping back in time to see her swallow.

"Damn, you taste good",

"You nasty bitch," they both laughed.

They have been fucking with each other for five years and have an open relationship. The rules are Thugga can fuck whoever he wants and as soon as he finds out Kiki is fucking someone else, she got her ass kicked.

"Whatever nigga, you love it and you know it."

Kiki got up to go to the bathroom and jump in the shower she came back and handed Thugga a wet washcloth to clean himself. Before she walked away he smacked her ass and watched it jiggle, it was so fat that it still turned him on after all these years.

"Be careful you asshole that hurts."

"Shut up I done gave that ass a harder beating then that before and hurry up in that shower I need you to go get my little niggas for me."

Thugga never spoke on the phone so calling his workers was a no no. He'd always send Kiki to get them; she's his ride or die partner and did whatever he needed. She's loyal and loves him, even though she knows love is far from his mind. Five years ago he saved her life and she would never let him down or betray him because of that. One night Kiki was being robbed by two crack heads, one pulled out a knife and that's when Thugga stepped in knocking out the crack head that held on to Kiki and shooting the other one in the chest. Kiki has been with him ever since, he turned her into one of the baddest bitches N.Y.C. has ever seen. She carried his drugs in and out of state, hold the guns, and wasn't afraid to use them. Thugga cleaned himself off put on his Polo boxer's and his Calvin Klein jeans, grabbed his book bag off the floor and started to empty the pack of cracks on the table just in time for Kiki to come out the shower dripping wet.

"Baby you seen the towels there's none in the bathroom."

"Want me to lick you dry?"

"Now who's the nasty bitch?"

"Whatever. They over there on the rack next to the closet."

Thugga watched as Kiki dried off. She's five foot two, double D's, small waist and a forty-five in the ass. Sometimes he couldn't believe how perfect her body was. She sat at the end of the bed, put her coco butter lotion on, her skin tight 7 jeans, no panties, and her top with no bra, she liked it that way, said it made her feel free under her clothes.

"You seen my heels daddy?"

"On my side of the bed" he said nodding his head in the direction of the shoes.

Kiki put her heels on, gave Thugga a kiss and left the hotel room. They never did business in the house, nor did they keep any drugs there, he started to count up the packs he put together for his runners. Thugga bought keys from the Columbians in Queens and instead of selling it whole sale he broke them down into 1,000 dollar packs. It took longer but he made more money. They rented a hotel room close to the Hillside projects they hustled out of on Boston Rd. in the Bronx so Kiki returned in no time followed by Dollar, Grav, Black, and Hussein. Thugga never turned around as they entered the room. Kiki took a seat on the bed and texted her friend Ruby Red while the men handled their business.

"Ya'll come in, find a seat" the boys did as they were told.

Each one of the boys got heart, that's the only reason Thugga fucked with them, but Thugga has a reputation of killing anyone who fucked with his money so they all had fear of him.

"What's poppin with you Thugga?"

"Aint shit Black, except for that money that's what's poppin."

"I can dig that" Black said grabbing the seat in front of Thugga to hear what the new plan was.

"Look like dis my niggas—this here—this the new shit we got, better then the last shit we had. I cooked it myself so you know its butter, have them crack heads licking they fingers like it was chicken" the boy's laughed, so did Kiki.

"Same plan, in each pack there's 1,000 dollars worth, you each take $200 off your pack and bring me back $800, that's $3,200 coming back to me, you got two day's any questions?"

"Nah" Grav said grabbing his pack.

"Yo! Thugga I gotta go, we aint had no work all day my phone been blowin' up, gotta go get this bread my nigga."

"I aint mad at you, get that money, and be safe out there young nigga." The boy's took their packs and started to roll out.

"Black—hold up. Let me holla at you."

"Whats good homie?"

"That money you brought me this morning, it was fuckin short." Black's eyes grew wide as Thugga looked him in his face with a look that could kill.

"A yo it wasn't me Thugga. And when you called me this morning you was in a hurry, when I collected from everybody I aint have time to count it"...Thugga just stared at him. Black is his lieutenant and been with Thugga for years and never came up short.

"Keep a closer eye on them niggas. When you find out who it is let me know, I'll take care of it myself."

"Aight" Black left the room thankful that Thugga believed him or else he would have died right there in that hotel room.

"You believe him daddy?"

"He never lied to me before, you ready?"

"Yep. Where we going?"

"Shopping".

# Chapter 3

*Kiki*

Thugga and Kiki went to the mall on a shopping spree they bought everything. Gucci, Prada, Fendi, Armani, shoes, shades, suits, dresses, jeans—whatever they wanted. They did this once a month every month. The way he looked at it, Kiki deserved everything she wanted for the things she did for him. He was proud of her, he gave her the game and she took it and instead of being just like him she found her own swagger. The bitch always stayed cool, never talked much when they were around Thugga's people and would kill any nigga who got in the way of what Thugga wanted to do.

"What we doing tonight daddy?"

"You got some work to do."

"What's good talk to me" she replied.

"There's this nigga from Brooklyn, my connect put me on to him. He robbed the connect for five birds so sun gave me the address, said I can keep whatever I get."

"How do I get to him?"

"Sun some soft dick nigga, do anything for some pussy so the way I see it, when he see your fat ass he'll be all over you. You know what to do."

They walked out the mall in silence. Kiki waited in front of the mall while Thugga pulled up in his all black Range Rover, one of his many whips. He also owned a Bentley GT, Maserati Granturismo, Audi R8 and his newest baby a Mercedes Benz S600.

They got home and put the clothes away. The whole ride Kiki hadn't said a word. Thugga was in the living room smoking a blunt and playing a video game when Kiki dropped to her knees in front of him, undid his pants, pulled his dick out and started to stroke it. She put half of him in her mouth letting the head of his dick tickle the back her throat. He grabbed the back of her head letting the remote hit the floor and started to pump his dick in and out of her mouth. Kiki loves to suck his dick, it made her cum just to see how much he enjoyed it. He drove his dick deep in her mouth; she gagged as Thugga came in her mouth. She swallowed it all, licked her lips, stood up and got undressed.

"My turn daddy" Kiki laid on the couch as Thugga put her legs on his shoulder and started to let his tongue dance around her clit before putting his mouth around her fat pussy causing her to cum instantly.

"Now hit it from the back pleeeease!" Kiki put that fat ass up in the air. Her pussy was already soaking wet so Thugga grabbed her hips and rammed his dick up in her.

"Yessss!" Kiki bit her bottom lip as he stroked her. This is what she wanted, a good hard fuck.

She started to moan in pleasure, closing her eyes feeling like she was in ecstasy as her legs got weak and she came harder than she ever had in her life, just then Thugga came inside of her. They both collapsed on the bed just laying there breathing hard.

"What time do I have to leave daddy?"

"In an hour."

Kiki jumped in the shower, lotion her body and got dressed in the all white Gucci dress Thugga bought her.

"How do I look daddy?" she asked doing a little spin for him to see.

Thugga looked her up and down smiling at how perfect the dress hugged her curves.

"Amazing" he told her getting up from the couch hugging her and kissing her deeply as he held on to her face with both hands.

"You got your clean up bag?"

"In my coach bag."

"Be careful out there, I don't know what I would do without you."

"I will daddy...I love you", Kiki said not really expecting an answer. She knew he wouldn't say it back, he never does; instead he kissed her lips one more time and smacked her on her ass as she walked away.

"How will I recognize him?" she asked over her shoulder.

"Black ugly nigga, got a tattoo on the left side of his neck says God's Son."

Kiki left the house grabbing the keys to the Range Rover off the table, she got in the truck looking in her bag and pulled out the paper Thugga gave her with the name and address on it.

"God's Son—get ready to meet your farther".

She started up the truck hitting the highway to Brooklyn, it only took her 25 minutes and she was pulling up in front of the building. She jumped out of the truck and popped the hood. It was still early morning so she was hoping it wouldn't take all day. It was in the middle of July, warm out, with a little wind blowing and she hoped her and Thugga could go to the park and hang out later. The front door to the apartment building she was standing in front of opened as she jumped into action like the Range Rover had broken down.

"Oh what am I gonna do, this thing just won't start."

"Excuse me miss can I help you?" Kiki turned around to see a light skinned brother standing in front of her.

"Oh nah I'm good" she said disappointed. She knew by the description that it wasn't Gods Son.

"I know a lot about cars, I'm pretty sure I can help you."

"Look I'm okay lil' nigga why don't you get the fuck out of here" dude gave Kiki a nasty look and walked away. "I aint got patients for this shit I shoulda smoked some of that blunt with Thugga, calm my fucking nerves." She heard the door open again this time she bent over to look in the truck, all Gods Son could see is her sexy fat ass bent over and no panties underneath. Kiki's 130 pounds, all hips, thighs and ass. God's Son's dick got hard instantly as he walked up on Kiki hoping she could see his dick print in his pants.

"What's poppin' shorty you need some help?" Kiki could smell the weed and alcohol on his breath and thought to herself 'shit! Aint it too early to drink' as she turned around and took a look at Gods Son. The first thing she looked at was the tattoo on his neck, when she was sure she had the right nigga she smiled.

"Oh thank God. I don't know what happened, I was driving and all of a sudden it just stopped." She said in an innocent voice. Gods Son was shocked when she turned around, he hadn't expected her to be so beautiful.

"Okay let me take a look sweetheart" he put his hands on the truck, looked around a little bit but couldn't find anything wrong. "Do me a favor, start it up let me see what's going on." As Kiki walked around the truck to the driver's side he couldn't believe how perfect the body on this young bitch was. She put the key in the ignition and started the truck up. She jumped out of the truck and jumped up and down clapping her hands like some dumb blond.

"Oh god I can't believe you fixed it", she cut the truck off, ran around the front, and gave Gods

Son a hug. He was taller than she was so she had to jump in his arms; she pulled back and gave him a kiss on the cheek all the time felling his hard dick against her stomach. She let him go but he held on to her waist "what's your name handsome?"

"They call me big G" he lied.

"Well big G, I got a long ride back to Harlem would you mind if I used your bathroom to freshen up before I get on the road?"

"Sure let me close this hood for you" as he closed the hood of the truck.

Kiki just shook her head. She couldn't believe how easy this nigga was, 'and he's suppose to be about something' she thought to herself.

"Let me grab my bag and lock up ok baby."

"Sure lil' mama go head." God's Son watched her grab her bag out the passenger side and locked the truck door 'imma tear that pussy the fuck up' he thought to himself.

"Ready?"

"Yeah" he opened the building door for her. "Im on the first floor, 1A" he let her go first, licking his lips and undressing Kiki with his eyes. She looked so perfect in her dress he couldn't wait to get her naked. He opened the door to his apartment and let them in. He had a nice apartment; you could tell he lives the life of a bachelor. He had all types of liquor in the kitchen, pornos in the living room, and condoms next to his weed on the table he should be eating his food on. If he lived with a bitch there would be no way all this shit would be in plain view.

"Oh this is nice, you got taste I love the leather couch—Italian?"

"But of course, nothing but the best" Kiki put her purse down on the table next to the condoms and the weed.

"I guess you were about to have a party huh?" she asked as her eyes combed the room looking for a safe, some jewelry, anything worth taking with her when she leaves.

"Nah, why you say that?"

"The weed."

"Always got good weed around."

"The liquor?"

"Like to drink."

"Condoms and pornos."

"Might have a girl around who likes to watch pornos and fuck" Kiki picked up the pack of condoms.

"Magnums huh?"

"Like I said baby, only the best."

"The question is, can you fit those?"

"Let's find out" Gods Son said coming closer to her.

"Be patient" Kiki said stepping back. "Where's your bathroom?" Gods Son pointed coming closer. "And your bedroom?" she said still stepping back. "Be a good boy and wait for me in there. I gotta go freshen up." Kiki grabbed her bag off the table, got on her tippy toes and gave him a kiss. He just watched as her ass swayed back and forth on her way to the bedroom. Kiki stopped, looked back and licked her lips before closing the bathroom door.

"I know that pussy good" he said as he grabbed his dick, a pack of condoms and went to his room. Meanwhile Kiki was in the bathroom going through her Coach bag. She pulled out what she and Thugga called a 'clean up' bag. It consists of rope, gloves, a mask, masking tape, a knife, a nine millimeter, extra bullets and a non-traceable phone just in case she wanted to call Thugga. She put the gloves on, cocked the gun, and placed it back in her bag. By the time she walked in his room he was lying on his bed naked, stroking himself.

"Ooooh look at that big dick, I can't wait to get that thing in my mouth." Kiki dropped her bag, then her dress. He couldn't believe his eyes, he's had plenty of bitches before but Kiki has the sexiest body he has ever seen. Fuck buffy, Vida, and Coco, this was a body like no other. Kiki walked to the bed seductively, then stepped on the bed and looked down at God's Son. "Bad bitches don't give up pussy, you gotta earn it" without another word, without warning Kiki squatted over and sat in his face. 'This nasty ass nigga' she thought to herself. He didn't know her from anywhere but started to eat her pussy like he was in love. "Yeah that's right nigga eat a bitch pussy and eat it good fuck boy!" That seemed to turn him on because he was now eating Kiki's ass. "Ooooh nigga yeah, oh you nasty huh!? I got something for your freaky ass". She made her way to her Coach bag and pulled out a rope.

"What you bout to do with that bitch?"

"Tie your hands up, suck your dick, fuck you silly and give you a fat nut." The look on God's Son said he wasn't sure about that. "What happen nigga you scared? Oh man I'm outta here you ol' soft ass nigga." Gods Son took one look at that ass walking away and said to himself 'fuck no I need that pussy.'

"Yo! Come here bitch, aint nobody scared of nothing." Kiki smiled knowing that would work then turned around and headed for the bed.

"That's what I'm talking about nigga, let's do this." Kiki tied him up as he licked his lips. "Yeah now let me get that fat pussy."

"Nah not yet."

"What?"

"You were being a bad boy, you didn't want me to tie you up in the first place so now you get punished" Kiki stepped back on the bed and squatted as Gods Son opened his mouth and stuck his tongue out inviting Kiki's warm pussy back in his mouth. Instead of giving him her juices, she gave him a golden shower. She pissed all in his mouth and all over his face.

"What the fuck you doing bitch!?" he said almost choking, "Oh you nasty ass bitch." Gods Son jumped off the bed as KIKI ran for her Coach bag pulling out her gun.

"Slow down fat boy."

31

"Hold on shorty, take it easy, you might just fuck around and hurt somebody with that you feel me." Gods son had his hands held out in prayer position piss dripping down his face.

"Shut the fuck up and lay your ass back down on that bed you big bitch."

"Yo! Look, it aint even got to go down shady shorty, just tell me what you want."

"Where's the fucking money?"

"In the closet, all the money you want, just put the fucking gun down ok." Kiki pulled the trigger leaving Gods Son's brains all over the bed. She didn't have time to waste, it was still early, people should be at work but you might never know who might have heard the shots. She ran to the closet tossing his clothes behind her.

"Fuck! Come on where are you?" when the racks were empty she bent down, the first bag she grabbed was heavy, when she opened it there was two glock nines in it, she tossed them to the side. Thugga would love them but that's not what she came for. She opened the last two boxes, "jack pot."

# Chapter 4

*Tiffany*

Tiffany opened the door to her apartment happy to be home after work, it was another long day at school and she was tired as hell. She locked the door behind her dropping her school bag and briefcase on the couch and went straight to her room. She was tired of coming home to no one. Never anyone there to greet her with open arms, it was nights like this she missed Jermaine. She undressed, got her things ready, and jumped in the shower. After she got out she lotion her body and admired her figure in the mirror. She loves her body and wish she had a man to enjoy it too. She picked up her phone and called her best friend, her only friend.

"Hello"

"Tina what's up?"

"Aint shit bitch what up with you?"

"I hate it when you call me bitch."

"I hate it when you act stuck up." Tina's been friends with Tiffany since elementary school.

They met when a group of girls were making fun of Tiffany's hair and right before she was about to cry Tina jumped in. "Hey why don't ya'll try that with me. I bet I'll beat all ya'll up." They were seven then, Tina's still feisty but now more about niggas, cash, cars, and dick more than fighting.

"I am not stuck up."

"Uh huh, that's why you single bitch, if you would loosen up and give a nigga some pussy you wouldn't be alone" Tiffany got quiet.

"Man I'm sorry Tiff, you know I aint mean it like that."

"No.....no it's ok. To be honest I kinda called you for some advice.

"Bitch you bout to get some dick aint you?"

"No! I'm not bout to go get no dick"

"So what's good Tiff? Stop keeping me in suspense."

"My mom."

"She's trying to send you on another blind date?"

"Yeah"

"And?"

"Well today for the first time in a long time I'm finding myself getting tired of being alone."

"Tiff! Go for it."

"You think so?"

"Yeah, now stop wasting time, call me later and tell me how it goes" before Tiffany could say anything Tina hung up. Tiffany put on her panties and bra, lay in the bed and called her mom.

"Hey baby you ok?"

"Hey mom. Uhm, I'm glad you're still up..."

"Give me a minute I'll get his number for you." Tiffany banged her fist against the bed. She was upset that her mother knew her that well. "You ready baby?"

"*Yes mom.*"

"718 555-2223 his name is Tyrese."

"Thanks mom, I love you."

"I love you too baby."

Tiffany hung up the phone and took a deep breath, "Damn what's wrong with you girl, your just calling a man, stop acting like you're about to break the law and just do it Tiffany."

"Ring, ring, ring."

"Yo hello"

"Yeah hi, is this Tyrese?"

"Yeah this is him, may I ask whose calling?"

"Yeah, this is Tiffany. My mom met you today and..."

"Oh yeah, nice lady that miss Jones, she told me so much about you. I'm so happy you called, how are you?"

"I'm fine and you?" As they spoke for a next hour Tiffany felt good inside to have someone to talk to other than Tina. She loves Tina to death but it felt good to hear a man's voice.

"Wow, I really enjoy your conversation Tiffany."

"Me too Tyrese, I really don't get to do this very much, I mean not because I'm not attractive, I get men who try to talk to me all the time, it's just I don't think many men are sincere.

"I feel you—hey Tiffany?"

"Yes."

"There's this little restaurant down the block from where I live, and well, I'd love to buy you dinner, what do you say?"

She hesitated for a second, "Sure Tyrese I'd really love that. Can you give me about an hour to get dressed?"

"Yeah, take all the time you need okay, I guess I'll see you soon."

"Cool, bye." Oh my god, what the fuck am I going to wear. Tiffany jumped off her bed and ran to her closet, she looked through everything and for the first time in a long time she noticed she didn't own anything sexy. Everything in her closet looked like it could only be worn to school or work; "shit" she turned around and looked at all her clothes on the floor. She finally spotted a white shirt she had bought but never wore because you could see right through it. "Sexy but too revealing...unless", she ran to her dresser draw and found a black bra to wear underneath and some all black tights she had planned to wear under her jeans to make her ass look firm. "Without the jeans he'll get a good look at my curves and go crazy." As she got dressed she stared at herself in the full length mirror in the living room, "you still got it girl." When she was sure she looked good she called Tyrese back, got the address of the restaurant and called a cab. This was her first date in two years and she was more than nervous, her palms were sweating, she had butterflies in her stomach and was shaking her legs, "calm down girl what's wrong with you?"

The cab pulled up in front of the restaurant, she called Tyrese and he told her what table he was sitting at and what he was wearing. As she entered the dinner she saw him standing and waving to her. 'He aint the cutest, but thank God he aint ugly.'

"Hi Tyrese."

"Hey Tiffany, you look good" he said looking her over and giving her a hug and a kiss on her cheek, 'a little too much but okay I guess' she thought about the kiss.

"Thank you, you look quite handsome yourself."

"Please, please, take a seat", they both sat down and Tyrese handed her a menu. "Please order whatever you want."

"Thank you" Tiffany looked at the menu and didn't see anything she liked, when she looked up Tyrese was staring at her catching her by surprise. He quickly looked down at the menu hoping that she didn't feel weird. He never meant to stare; he was just admiring her beauty.

"See anything you like?"

"No not really."

"At the age of 15 I killed my farther" Tyrese said out of nowhere.

"What?"

"Yeah didn't do too much time for it tho, I was a juvenile, you know how that go" he said leaning back using his finger nail to clean out his teeth.

"Are you serious?"

"Yeah I was later diagnosed as being bi-polar so they sent me home you know, really wasn't in my right mind when I did it...oh, hold up." Tyrese dug in his pocket and came out with a pill bottle, opened it up and took one. "Guess I shoulda took that before the date, probably wouldn't have told you all that...So, we fuckin tonight or what?"

Thanks mom!

Visit us at www.brthewriter.com

# Chapter 5

"Wait daddy your hurting me" Ruby Red said as she was bent over the couch in the living room, her pussy was getting punished. She loved the way he fucked her, he always did it right. They would go at it for hours at a time, suckin and fuckin each other until they exploded all over the place. This time they started in the shower, then the bed; Ruby Red had no idea how they ended up in the living room but it was great—every second, minute, and hour of it.

"Shut the fuck up bitch, you ask for some dick now take it" he said grabbing her by her hair and smacking her hard on her ass.

"Oh word! It's like that? So you think you just gonna fuck me huh!" Ruby Red looked back and bit her bottom lip before she started to work her hips and grind all over his dick. They were both making so much noise it sounded like a mother fuckin porno in that bitch.

"Yeah bitch that's what I'm talking about"

"It feels good daddy?"

"Yeah now fuck me harder" Thugga said smacking Ruby on her ass. Her pussy was good but it wasn't fucking with Kiki, the only thing Ruby had over Kiki was Ruby sucks dick like one of them porn stars.

Three months ago Ruby Red had thrown herself at him and he couldn't resist the 5 foot 7 beauty. She stood at 155 pounds and legs so firm, sexy, and strong she could wrap them around you and trap your ass. She did nothing but squats every day. She had firm legs and a nice fat ass and right now she was working it against Thugga's dick.

"Fuck me, fuck me, fuck me", she repeated knowing it turned Thugga on to hear a bitch talk shit when he was fuckin. Thugga bust off in her pussy he pulled out and cum dripped all down her leg.

"You good daddy?"

"Yeah" he said smacking her on her ass one more time before stepping back and lying on the floor, he was out of breath and sweating.

"Shit was that good" Ruby didn't say anything she just laid there in that position smiling, glad that he enjoyed himself hoping that she was better than all his other bitches.

"Why you be fucking me like that?"

"Because the pussy good, head good, and no matter what nigga you fuck with you always gonna remember me."

"Is it better than Kiki?"—Thugga took a deep breath jumped up and put his boxers on. He reached for his pants and pulled out his cigarette, lit it, took a deep pull, leaned his head back and blew the smoke out like he was releasing some type of stress. He was tired of bitches trying to compare themselves to Kiki and refuse to answer her.

"Let's get down to business."

"Fuck you Thugga."

"Whatever, just put your clothes on and get in the fucking kitchen." Thugga had come over to get her to cook the last five keys he had stashed at her house. Ever since he started fucking with Ruby he taught her how to cook large amounts of coke. He's gonna break down enough to double his money and give it to his soldiers, and with the rest he decided it's time to start selling weight. With what Kiki was about to bring back, he should make enough money to buy keys and keep his blocks

43

running. He was about to be bigger than he ever dreamed...and he couldn't wait.

"Thugga pass me that coffee pot and the baking soda under the sink so I can make magic." Ruby had gotten dressed ignoring Thugga's comment and was ready to get down to business. She hated being the chick on the side and tried her best to please him and figured if she did everything he asked, one day he would see how she really felt about him. Ruby's a bad bitch and could have any nigga she wanted but Thugga was it in her eyes.

"Here you go, you need anything else or can I go in the shower and wash you off my balls before Kiki smells you all over me?"

"Go head boy." Ruby said laughing as she took out the scissors and carefully cut the package of the first kilo open and emptied it into a pan. She used the measuring cup to make sure she didn't put too much baking soda in the coke. Once she was done she threw it in the pot, turned the fire on, hit the play button on the remote so that Young Jeezy blared through the speakers and began to cook. In no time she had all the coke cooked and ready for Thugga to do his thing. He came out the bathroom fully dressed.

44

"Hey baby girl, I gotta run!

"Is everything ok?" she asked.

"Yeah, Kiki home with that shit and Dollar just called me said it was important so I'll go see him first. I'll be back tomorrow" he said giving her a kiss.

Follow me at Twitter.com/@brthewriter

# Chapter 6

*Black*

"Hey what's poppin shorty you absolutely beautiful, God damn look at that ass," Black's a hot boy, loves women and hustling. If you let him tell it he's been hustling his whole life. But one thing's for sure, he does it well. That's why Thugga made him lieutenant, and the fact that Black wasn't afraid to bust his gun, so Thugga knew he would hold the block down.

 "What's good with ya'll niggas?" Black asked his crew as he pulled up giving them all pounds.

"What's poppin homeboy, fuck you been at?" Dollar asked.

"Getting my dick wet."

"Word, who Lexy?"

"Nah I'm tired of fucking that bitch, I bagged that bad bitch Crystal this morning."

"Say word!" Grav asked jumping off the crate he was sitting on. They were on the corner of Fish Ave. and Boston Rd. "I been tryin to fuck that bitch forever."

47

"Yes sir she got some good pussy too nigga", Black said rubbing his hands together.

"Fuck you Black word up yo! Plug me in with that bitch."

"I got you, breathe easy tho here she come" he put niggas on point nodding his head in her direction.

"Hi Black" Crystal said in a sexy voice as she walked by with a group of friends, "had fun this morning?"

"And you know it" Black answered licking his lips.

"A yo! Crystal, who's your homegirl?" Hussein asked. She was walking with two friends they've never seen before.

"They don't like drug dealers."

"Damn it's like that Crystal?" Dollar said with an 'I can't believe you said that' look on his face.

"Im just playin Hussein, they Harlem bitches so you know they love a hustler."

"Well ya'll gonna love me" he yelled after them.

"Okay, okay, we got time for that later how we looking out here?" Black interrupted.

"Quiet. Police was out earlier fucking with niggas, we just played the store whenever they drove by tho." Grav told Black pointing back to the bodega they hustled in front of.

"Yeah it slowed paper down for a while but shit picked back up bout a half hour ago" Dollar said, now sitting on the crate Grav was on, "we should be finished with this pack Thugga gave us real soon."

"That's what's up, my nigga's gonna be happy to hear that" Black said checking his Rolex to see what time it is. They didn't call him Black because of his skin complexion. He was actually light skin; they called him black because it's his favorite color. He dressed in black from head to toe. "Yo! Their go paper who's it on?"

"Me." Dollar said jumping off the crate jogging to the car that just pulled up on the curve. There was a white boy they called Red in it.

"What's good Dollar?"

"What's up Red what you need?"

"Gimme ten dimes."

"Okay, hold up." Dollar looked up and down the street to see if the police was around before going in his sock to get the pack of crack. He took out ten dimes and gave them to Red in exchange for a hundred dollar bill. Red threw the dimes in his mouth, that way if the police was to pull him over he could swallow them instead of them finding it.

"I'll get with you guys later Dollar."

"Okay Red, drive safe and be easy" Dollar watched as Red pulled off and ran back to the fellas.

"Next one on you Grav."

"Ok homie good looking" Grav pulled out a dime bag of weed.

"Ooooh weeeee, what's that baby boy?" Hussein asked.

"That good shit, that mother fuckin white widow. I had to go all the way to Harlem for this kid." Hussein pulled out a dutch from his pocket and started to crack it.

"Yep! Put that in the air" Black said "Yo! Check it out right, that bitch Crystal, she a stone cold freak."

"Oh yeah, I gotta hear this shit." Grav said paying extra close attention, "Damn Black, tell the truth, that pussy good aint it?"

"That shit on fire" Black said giving Dollar a pound. Hussein took a few hits of the blunt and passed it to Black as he listened to the story "Yo! That lil' bitch was sucking a nigga nuts and all that, I fucked around and tea bagged that bitch"

"Hell nah say word my nigga."

"Word."

"And what she do?" Grav asked, Black took a hit of the blunt and blew the thick white smoke in the air.

"Nah nigga let me smack this sale first," Grav ran to the customer's car "what up?"

"Just two!" Grav watched the street for the police but all he could see was summer time in action; kids playing basket ball with crates they made into rims tied to a pole, little girls jumping rope, the ice cream truck, and old ladies in lawn chairs in front of their apartment buildings. Grav put his hands in his ass crack and came out with a bag of crack and gave the fiend two in exchange for $20 dollars, running back to hear the story "Aight what happened now?"

"Where was I at...oh yea, that bitch suck a mean dick, pussy get wetter than wet, and she talk shit my nigga."

"What you mean?"

"Damn Grav what you a virgin?"

"Nah, he aint no virgin, nigga just aint fucking pussy right. He aint never made a bitch scream, yell, or cum" the boys all laughed at Dollar's joke. They are all still teenagers so cracking on each other all day was still part of their daily routine.

"Yeah aight nigga, I'll make your bitch squirt tho."

"Yo Black, here that bitch come now." Black turned around and noticed Crystal had dropped off one of her friends, but the one coming back with her had so much hips and thighs that her ass had to be fat.

"What up Crystal, were ya'll headed?"

"Back to your house" Chrystal said giving Black a seductive look, "why you coming with us?" Black looked at Chrystal, then to her friend, and seen the same seductive look.

"Hell yeah, hold up tho," Black passed the blunt back to Hussein. "Yo! Dollar do me a favor sun, when everybody's finished, collect that bread for me and call that nigga Thugga, tell him to come collect that shit you heard.

"I heard! Have fun nigga."

"And you know it!" The boy's watched as Black walked away with Crystal and her friend. He was now in the middle of both the woman with his hands on their shoulders.

"I can't believe it" Grav said "this nigga gotta be the luckiest nigga alive bee."

"Yeah fuck all that, this is the perfect time to do what we been talking about the whole week. Ya'll niggas just stick to the plan ya' dig me?" Dollar pulled his cell phone out and called Thugga.

"Yo!"

"What's poppin big homie?"

"Me, why wassup?"

"Nah this nigga Black collected but he bounced with this bitch and told me to holla at you and give you the bread, but I got some news for you homie that I don't think you gonna like"

"Yeah...well not over the phone, I'll be there in a minute."

For any questions or concerns email us at

BR@BRTHEWRITER.COM

# Chapter 7

*Thugga*

When Thugga walked in the house Kiki was sitting on the couch smoking a blunt and watching a movie. She had a t-shirt on, no panties, and no bra. She knew after all the work she just put in Thugga was about to give her some dick, until she noticed the look on his face.

"What's good daddy?"

"Nothing. Give me a minute." Thugga went to the kitchen, got himself a cup and poured a shot of Henny before joining Kiki on the couch.

"How'd it go?"

"Just as planned, found little more than expected tho" Kiki said passing the blunt and then pulling a Gucci duffle bag from under the couch and poured everything out on the table. Thugga took one look at everything and nodded his head.

"That's a good fucking look, that fucking nigga had ten birds. How much bread in there?"

"You know I don't count your fucking money daddy."

"Get the machine for me." Kiki went to the closet and got the digital IBM money counter Thugga left there, she ran back excited about the lick knowing the money would make him happy. When she got back to the living room, Thugga had the same look on his face he did when he first walked through the door.

"Baby what's wrong?"

"Black."

"Is he ok?" Kiki asked sounding worried.

"The fuckin bitch ass nigga is the one that been shorting the money."

"Nah" Kiki said in disbelief "no not Black?!"

"Shit, how you think I feel if you reacting like that. This nigga been ridin with me for the longest, and now I find out he been stealing from me." Kiki knew the love Thugga had for his little lieutenant. Black was the rider he took to do everything with him, rob, steal, kill...whatever. And, Kiki knew it but never said anything but they even ran trains on bitches together.

"How'd you find out?"

56

"Dollar!"

"Is he sure?"

"Black gave him the money.He said it was short when he got it, Grav and Hussein witnessed it. Black tried to set Dollar up and cover for himself."

"Oh man what you gonna do daddy?"

"Kill him, later for that tho." Thugga remembered he had money to count and knew he would be in a better mood after. Kiki helped him dump the sneaker box out and pop the rubber band on the stacks of money. When they finished counting Thugga gave Kiki a nice soft kiss on her lips. Kiki had done well, she got ten birds and a hundred thousand dollars out of Gods Son. Thugga sat on the couch with Kiki sitting sideways in his lap "listen baby girl, I got a new plan."

"I'm down for whatever daddy."

"Imma rob the connect Paco."

"What" Kiki said shocked.

"Don't worry, got another connect lined up but with these ten birds, and this bread, if we could get our hand on what Paco got we could supply the whole N.Y. ya' dig?" Kiki smiled, seeing

Thugga's vision. "No more small time shit, we moving up weezzy" Kiki laughed at Thugga's joke. She loved him so much she's always willing to follow his lead. If Thugga jumped off a mountain she would jump too just because he said it was safe.

"You stupid...sounds good to me daddy, help me pack this shit up so I can get it out the house, Ruby should be waiting on me."

"Yeah ok, tell that bitch I said have the birds you give her to the side when I get there tomorrow. We gonna get rid of the five cooked ones and then we'll start to sell the raw, these niggas gotta cook up shit them fuckin selves. And remember in the morning I gotta go to the insurance place. Remind me cause I shoulda been went, I got a lot on my mind." Thugga lay back as he thought about murdering Black.

# Chapter 8

*Tiffany*

I got to work twenty minutes early which was cool, I wanted to call Tina and planned on using the job phone so I wouldn't have to run up my day time minutes.

"Ring ring ring."

"Hello." Tina answered the phone sounding like she was still asleep.

"Tina you sleep?"

"Nah bitch I just sound like this on the regular. What the fuck is wrong with you, you know I don't get the fuck up till 12:00 bitch, it's nine in the morning."

"I'm sorry girl, I just wanted to tell you about my date last night, but I'll call you back later"

"Fuck nah hoe, you aint had a date in 1,000 years let me hear bout this."

"Girl you won't believe it, this weirdo ass nigga is bipolar."

"Shut up!"

"No for real, he went on about how he killed his father and got away with it."

"Killed his dad?"

"Girl then the dude gonna ask me if we fuckin tonight or what." I told her as we both laughed. Then I couldn't believe what I saw coming my way. "Girl I gotta go, I got a client coming."

"Ok call me back tho I gotta hear the rest of this shit Tiffany."

I never got a chance to hear what Tina said, my eyes were fixed on the brother coming my way.

"Hey how you, I'm Sean Clark, I'm suppose to come in and sign some papers today for my car insurance". Before I answered I couldn't help but to study his six foot frame, he must have weighed 225 pounds, all muscle, chocolate brown skin, and when he smiled at me I almost melted. Today is the day I met Thugga and my life changed and would never again be the same—boy do I have a story to tell.

I looked into his eyes and saw something different, as if there was a story in them, a story I wanted to hear. He was confident but far from cocky. I reached my hand out for him to shake; it was firm, but tender all at the same time.

"Please Mr. Clark take a seat."

"Ok ma, good looking but you aint got to call me mister, you can call me Thugga."

"Okay Thugga" at that point I wondered if he told all the girls to call him Thugga or was I special. He stared at me, but not that kind of stare that weirdo mother fucker gave me last night, but more of a 'you and me belong together' kinda look. I blushed a little, smiled, and looked away from him; when I looked back he was smiling too. Oh my God was he handsome, his smile made my heart skip a beat "oh um, let me see" I finally said grabbing control of myself. "I have your folder right here, you're getting full coverage on a brand new S600 Mercedes Benz, is that right?" I asked him not wanting to look up from his folder, not wanting to look into his brown eyes afraid I might get lost in them.

"Yeah white on white", the sound of his voice sent chills through my body, gave me butterflies in my stomach. He spoke in a raspy voice, low but clear and even. I took a look at him, my attraction to him multiplied by ten.

This brother was different and I was gonna find out how.

"Did you drive the car here? I have to inspect it."

"Sure it's outside, come take a look sweetheart". Sweetheart—now I've been called that before, but coming out of his mouth it sounded totally different. I got up from my desk and noticed him looking over my body, it made me feel so sexy and I hoped he enjoyed what he saw. I had worn my favorite skirt to work thank God; it showed off my curves perfectly. He walked ahead of me so I could check out his body without him noticing. His arms were the biggest I've ever seen, his back was wide and strong; there was no mistake that this brother worked out hard. He had on a Prada contour t-shirt, black linen shorts and black Prada loafers. You can tell by his demeanor he was ruff and rugged, maybe even straight from the streets, but he had style and a touch of class that made him well rounded. When we got to his whip I was impressed. He had the Benz sittin on 22's, the white on white was clean, he didn't ruin it with TVs in the headrest like so many other niggas. Then I looked the car over to make sure there were no dents in it or no scratches to put in his folder.

"I never caught your name sweetheart."

"Oh my god I'm sorry my name is Tiffany, Tiffany Jones."

"Oh ok, I spoke to you yesterday, you're the one with the sexy voice."

"Yeah that was me" I said blushing remembering how I felt when he said he couldn't wait to meet me, "well everything seems fine here, shall we go in and sign these papers?"

"Yeah we good!" He let me walk in front of him this time. I knew he was watching my ass so I walked with all the sexuality my body possesses. We sat at my desk, I handed him the folder and watched him as he signed. He slid it back to me and stood up.

"Thank you Tiffany you have a good day lil' mama" he was leaving and I didn't know what to say, 'what's wrong with you Tiff, say something' I thought to myself, 'don't just let this man walk out of here'. Just when I was about to say something he turned around and gave me that smile, that smile that makes me melt, and as fast as he came he left. I dropped my head and cursed myself for being so stupid. When I looked at his file, by his signature he wrote, 'call me don't let your future pass you by'.

# Chapter 9

*Thugga*

I couldn't believe how beautiful that girl Tiffany is. It totally took me by surprise. I sat there trying to control myself but all the time I wanted to bend her over and fuck her right there on her desk.

Now I've fucked with a lot of bitches but there was something about Tiffany, something different. There was an innocence about her that turned me on. She wasn't as thick as I like them but she had a perfect figure none the less—Kiki had a fatter ass than she did, and bigger breast, but Tiffany's beauty was unlike any other I've ever seen. Her eyes, the way she looked at me was almost as if she could see my soul. Her lips were juice, I couldn't help but think how soft they were and couldn't wait to feel them around my dick—shit! 'Snap out of it Thugga you got business to take care of' I told myself. I was tired of playing the game and ready to own the team. I been selling drugs too long to be just surviving and by surviving I mean all the best gear, flyest cars and decked out apartments. I want houses, private jets to take me to the islands, and clothes I can't even pronounce. It's my time and I'm taking over today!

Then I remembered Black, how could he betray me, after all I've done for him? The fuckin nigga was young and homeless when I found his ass. His parents was on drugs and left the nigga on the street to die. I took him home and gave him a place to stay and taught him how to be the hustler he is today. The nigga moved out, got his own spot, a little beamer and this is how he repays me.

Thugga thought back to the summer morning five years ago. He had just ran some crack heads off the block who were hanging around. He knew they were tryin to steal his stash so he made an example out of them by beating both of them with a bat until they were almost unconscious.  He ran up in the project buildings just in case someone seen him and called the police when he heard someone creeping up behind him. He spun around ready to knock whoever it was head off. When he turned around he was face to face with a young boy no older than 15.

"Yo! Chill dog"

"Man shorty what the fuck you doing creeping up on a nigga with a bat in his hand for?!"

"I wasn't creeping, I seen the blood on the bat and decided to get out of here."

"Go head scary ass little nigga" Thugga moved out the way letting lil' man go by. Lil' man walked by him and out the building. Thugga looked out the door just in time to see a cop grab the lil' nigga.

"Hey what you doing out here by yourself son?"

"Uhh um, I'm on my way to school" the officer let him go, all the time watching his face for the slightest sign that he was lying.

"Someone called the police—said there was a disturbance in the area, did you see who did that to those two poor men?" the cop pointed in the direction of the two men Thugga just got finished beating. They were still laying there unconscious.

"Shit" Thugga whispered to himself. He was sure that the lil' nigga he just scared was gonna rat on him.

"Nah, I aint see nothing" Thugga blew out the air he was holding in out of relief after he saw the lil nigga shake his head, when the cop walked away he called lil' man back into the building.

"A yo!, shorty come here bee" he looked back at Thugga, then checked to make sure the cop wasn't watching before running back in the building "yo what's your name homie?"

"Tyrone."

"Tyrone huh" Thugga dipped in his pocket and came out with a hundred dollar bill and handed it to Tyrone, "that was some brave shit you did you know that?"

"Thanks."

"You need a ride to school or something?" Tyrone lowered his head.

"Nah I'm good."

"Whats poppin shorty, what's wrong?" Thugga didn't push the issue he just stood there waiting on Tyrone to answer.

"My mom and dad left me, I've been living out here for two weeks getting by the best way I could" he grabbed his shirt "I wasn't trying to go to school with the same shit on everyday—bitches wasn't gonna laugh at me." Thugga had to smile, here this little nigga was telling him he was homeless and all he could think about was what the bitches will think.

"That's fucked up homie. If I were you I'd take that money I just gave you and buy some food, find a place to rest your head tonight and whatever you got left get some gear—get fresh lil' nigga and go to school, a mind is a terrible thing to waste" Thugga said while walking by him to look out the door. He made sure the police was gone and broke out while he had a chance. He ran to the car and started it up. When he looked up he saw Tyrone walking out the building, head down and the same look on his face he had when Thugga asked him if he needed a ride to school.

"Shit!" Thugga rolled down the window and yelled at Tyrone. "A yo lil'nigga come on—and hurry up man" Tyrone smiled, ran over to the car and jumped in.

"Good looking big homie". That was years ago, since then he's raised Black, and this betrayal, he never seen coming.

The phone rang snapping me out of my thoughts. I picked up the phone and a cold look came across my face when I realized who it was. I put Black on speaker.

KITTY KAT CREW

A Novel by B.R.

Coming soon.

# Chapter 10

*Black*

"What?"

"What? What you mean what? You good big homie?" I asked Thugga.

"Yeah I'm straight, talk to me I'm short for time."

"Yo Thugga you gotta get over to my crib nigga I got these freak bitches Crystal and her home girl over here giving me a threesome."

"I don't want none of your bitches nigga."

"Yo! Whats poppin? Whats good with you big homie?"

"We got work to put in and your ass is over there having threesomes that's what's wrong with me, be at my house at nine nigga" Thugga said hanging up the phone.

'Damn somebody got him pissed' I thought to myself thinking back not being able to remember Thugga ever speaking to me like that. "Yo! Ya"ll bitches gotta go" I told crystal and her friend putting my phone down. When I turned around Chrystal and her home girl was lying on the bed kissing, playing with each other's clits.

"But we're not finished yet daddy."

"I said get dressed and get the fuck out!" I yelled scaring the girls. I watched as they jumped up and quickly got dressed. On their way out Crystal looked back, "damn Black I jump out there and find a bitch to give you a threesome and this is how you treat a bitch?" I didn't answer, a few seconds later I heard my apartment door slam. I decided to smoke a cigarette before I jumped in the shower and washed these two bitches juices off my balls. Damn they were good but all I could think about was why Thugga was upset, shit if a nigga fucked with my big homie I'll kill a nigga. I took another pull of my cigarette and remembered the day Thugga brought me home.

Thugga opened the door to his apartment and let Tyrone in "you hungry lil' nigga?"

"Yeah and thirsty you got anything to drink?"

"What you want?"

"Some Kool-Aid." When Thugga went to the kitchen to get the drink Tyrone couldn't help but to let his eyes wonder. He couldn't believe how Thugga was living, flat screens everywhere, leather couches and one of the baddest bitches Tyrone has ever seen walking to the living room.

"Thugga! Thugga!?"

"What up? What the fuck you yelling for?"

"Who dis in the middle of our living room daddy?"

"This is Tyrone he's gonna be staying with us for a while. Tyrone this is my bitch Kiki."

"Oh ok, what's shakin' Tyrone?" Tyrone didn't know what to say, he was just stuck on Kiki's beauty. Thugga smacked Tyrone in the back of his head.

"Lesson number one, never fall victim to a fat ass and a pretty face. These bitches will ruin your life if you let them."

"Thugga stop trying to corrupt that boy's mind "Kiki said giving her man a hug and kiss, "how'd shit go today?"

"Had to put some work in, almost got knocked but Tyrone here looked out for a nigga" Thugga told Kiki as he handed Tyrone some Kool Aid and an iced honey bun, Kiki's favorite.

73

"Thank you for making sure my man came home safe Tyrone."

"You're welcome." Thugga taught Tyrone everything, how to hold and shoot a gun, how to bag up crack, and how to make a bitch come. Whenever Thugga took Kiki and Tyrone shopping he noticed Tyrone would pick out everything black, so he gave him the name Black.

As I jumped in the shower I couldn't help but to have this feeling like something was terribly wrong. Call it God trying to send me a message or just hustler's intuition but something was wrong. I jumped out the shower and got dressed. Black jeans, black hoodie, hustler gear, killer gear, it fit my mood. I took one last look at myself before jumping in the beamer, pumped some old Tupac and smoked a blunt while I drove; a habit of mine. I got to Thugga's crib in no time we hustled in the Bronx but lived in Mount Vernon just off the border line. If you cross 241 St. into 242nd and White Plains Rd. you leave the Bronx and you're in Mount Vernon just like that. I parked the car and noticed someone peeking out of Thugga's window. He lived on the first floor, always did. He says if it ever gets funky for any reason he could jump out the window and make a run for it without worrying about breaking his legs. When I got inside everybody was there. Kiki, Ruby Red, Dollar, Grav, Hussien and Thugga

with this look on his face, one I know all too
well, one that say's someone's about to die.

"Glad you can join us Black."

"Sorry I'm late didn't know we were having a
meeting."

"Yeah" Thugga said sarcastically "aight look
ya'll, it's a new day we coming up in the world."
I took a seat on the couch next to Ruby Red
everyone was positioned in a small circle with
Thugga sitting in one of those reclining chairs
"from now on I'll be selling weight so
everybody's position bout to change. I don't
need these blocks no more so imma make ya'll
bosses" as the words came out his mouth you
seen everyone's reaction, nigga's was smiling,
some sat back others leaned in to pay closer
attention "Dollar you got Fish Ave."

"That's what I'm talking bout."

"Grav you got Wilson"

"Good looking big homie" Grav said already
imagining the money he was about to make
and the different type of bitches that was gonna
be attracted to him knowing he was a boss, he
even thought about taking Crystal away from
Black.

"Hussein you got Corsa Ave. The catch to this is ya'll gonna buy weight from me and only me. If I hear ya'll bought weight from someone else imma kill you, straight music." Thugga looked around the room to make sure he had everybody's attention and that they understood.

"Kiki you got the same job droppin off the weight to niggas it gotta get to, but imma also give you Seymore Ave. so you can get you a group of bitches to sell weed for you, no hard shit understand?"

"Yes daddy" Kiki couldn't believe it, she was gonna finally have her own shit, own drugs, own money, own block, she could finally stand on her two and not depend on Thugga for money.

"Ruby Red you'll continue to cook that butter up" I can tell Ruby was heated that that's all she got. No boss roll like everyone else but she forced a smile on her face "Okay homie you know I got you"

"Black" Thugga just stared at me for a moment "you gonna stay by my side, I need a stick up kid with me at all times, never know when it gotta go down."

"I'm with you homie" was all I could say but in my mind I was flipping. I couldn't believe it, he made these soft ass pussy niggas that five minutes ago were under me bosses and I was a stick up kid I felt disrespected and let down by the man who raised me.

"Our first move go down tonight, the nigga I buy weight from Paco, we gonna take him for all he's worth, everybody got the money they owe me?" Thugga watched as Dollar went in his pocket and pulled out the remainder of what he didn't collect last night. Thugga took the money and gave it to Kiki "Use that money to buy your first 8 pounds of piff. I need everybody out except for Black, Kiki got one key of coke for each one of you niggas I'll give it to you for 25 a key since the first one is on consignment bring me back 30, and start coppin from there dig me?" Everybody nodded their heads letting Thugga know they understood. He watched as Kiki handed them the duffle bags each containing one kilo of coke. The house emptied out all except for Kiki. She went to her bed room to count her money and call her weed connect from Washington Heights to put her order in. I wondered if I should say something to Thugga about how I was feeling about my new position and decided to go head until Thugga cut me off "you got a gun with you Black?"

"Nah you aint tell me what was poppin, didn't know I needed one." Thugga got up from his seat went to the back of the house and came

back with two glock nines putting one in his
waist and tossing me the other.

# Chapter 11

*Paco and Black*

The traffic to Queens on the highway was heavy so we were stuck for a good twenty minutes and I decided that this was a better time than any to holla at him.

"A yo Thugga, you mad at me homie?" Thugga just looked at me for a moment without an answer.

"Why you ask me that my nigga? You did something I should be mad about?"

"Nah that's why I can't understand why you treating me like some nobody nigga."

"Nah never that scrap, I just got a lot on my mind that's all, shit we bout to rob and kill a nigga you aint nervous?"

"Oh yeah you right", right then and there I knew Thugga was lying to me, as many times as we robbed a nigga, as many times as I seen him kill a nigga, I've never seen him nervous.

"Hold up tho let me call this nigga Paco"

"Ring, ring, ring,"

"Hello" a deep Columbian accent came through the phone.

"Paco what up dog?"

"Nothing, just home relaxing watching Columbia beat Jamaica in the world cup soccer game."

"Check it out Paco there's something I need to talk to you about, I'll be there in twenty minutes"

"Good" Paco hung up, Thugga let the window down tossing the throw away phone out the window, he never called from his phone all the police had to do was pull up his phone records and see who was the last person who he spoke to and that's exactly what he didn't want. No connections to him and the dirt he did to others. We ended up making it to Paco's house in fifteen minutes; he lived in the suburbs of Queens. The neighborhood was quiet; only white people lived out here, and that worried me, shit, for all I know these crackers could spot us and call the police just off G.P. but I trust Thugga he always knows what he's doing.

"Ready lil' bro?"

"Yea I'm good" I said tapping the pistol on my waist Thugga gave me. "This shit is nice" I was talking about Paco's house, shit was all white, two floors, grass in the front yard, and a two car garage. Thugga has never brought anyone here.

"Who is your friend Thugga?" When I looked up I seen a pale skinned man waiting in the entrance to the house, slick back hair like he had gel in it, dress shirt open at the top, some slacks on and some dress shoes, real mob shit for a nigga chillin at the crib. Paco kinda reminded me of Jacob the jeweler in the face.

"Paco this is my son black, his mother sent him to live with me, he just finished school."

"Congratulations Black!"

"Thank you" Thugga and Paco hugged like two old friends, he shook my hand and showed us in. Paco was living good, his living room was so big the nigga had enough room to put a Jacuzzi in the middle of it. Crystal everything, he had everything from chandeliers to mink carpets, which we weren't allowed to go close to with shoes on, big screens everywhere and a black cat so big the shit coulda been a panther for all I know. He explained it was a rare cat from another country...whatever. Then to top it off two naked white bitches ran pass me and jumped in the Jacuzzi.

"Please, take your shoes off let's sit in the living room and talk business while I watch my girl's—Kelly can't swim" we laughed at his joke even though it wasn't funny. When I looked behind Paco the girl's were in the Jacuzzi kissing.

"Nah I aint got time for that" Thugga said pulling out his glock, so I pulled out mine. Paco looked at Thugga and narrowed his eyes.

"You fucking nigger, all I've done for you and this is what you do?"

"Shut the fuck up, where's the stash nigga?"

"This is my house you really think I would keep shit here?"

"Pat him down Black, he be having a 38 revolver in an ankle holster" I patted Paco down and found the 38 right where Thugga said.

"You know me well"

"Where's the stash?"

"In a safety deposit box" Thugga aimed the glock at the bitches in the hot tub, they were still making out like they were on coke, a ecstasy pill or something, they had no idea what was happening as Thugga pulled the trigger twice killing them both, Paco never turned around instead he looked at Thugga calmly.

"You've gone too far don't you think?"

"I'm gonna ask you one more time where is it?"

"There's a picture in my bedroom of those two naked girls on the wall" Paco said talking about the two dead bitches "There's a safe behind it"

"What's the combination?"

"3478" Thugga flew up the stairs to check the safe I put the 38 I got off of Paco on my waist and had the glock pointed at his dome. Thugga came back to my side with three garbage bags full to the top and gave the head nod in my direction, I already knew what I had to do. Without hesitation I shot Paco in the head, the blast from the glock was loud so I looked at Thugga and told him "Yo! Let's get out of here kid!"

"Nah doggy, only one of us is leaving here." Thugga had raised his gun at me, he didn't shoot he just pointed it and stared I thought to myself this nigga must be fuckin stupid he acting like I aint a "G" like I aint gonna bust too. I raised my gun hand quick and pulled the trigger, this fuckin crazy ass nigga didn't even move, he aint blink or nothing just stood there, smiling. I realized then my life was over, Thugga gave me a gun with one bullet in it, and I used it to kill Paco. How could I have been so stupid? How could I have not checked the clip? Because the gun was given to me by my supposed to be homie, my mentor, the only man I've ever killed for, the only man I've ever loved, that's why. Well I can tell you one thing; it's not like the movies. A nigga get shot and die instantly. Shit! That bullet hit my head and I felt my forehead crack. I could feel my blood exploding and trickling down my face as I was falling backward then the back of my head hit the ground with a hard crashing, cracking sound. I guess that was the back of my head shattering or maybe the bullet coming out, whatever it was I felt no more pain my body was now numb. I shook a bit, not like I was cold, but more like my nerves was breaking down. I shitted on myself, I couldn't feel it but the smell was undeniable. As I stared up at the ceiling I seen Thugga walk over me he shook his head and said something, I couldn't hear him, and then the fight was over. I took a deep breath as if I was stressed or tired and that's the last thing I'll ever remember...

# Chapter 12

*Tiffany*

I couldn't keep my mind off Thugga. Ever since I met him this morning he was all I could think about. I hadn't been able to concentrate at work that day and decided to skip school and was pacing my living room wondering if I should call him. I like the name Thugga and decided to call him that instead of Sean. I picked up the phone and decided to call and hung up. Oh God suppose he turns out to be a weirdo like that guy from last night—no impossible he's too fine to be crazy 'just do it tiffany' I thought to myself.

"Ring, ring, ring,"

"Yo!"

"Hello Thugga?" The phone got quiet for a second too long, my heart started pumping as I looked at the phone to see if he hung up.

"Yeah who dis?"

"This is tiffany from the insurance company"

"Yeah I gotta call you back"

85

"Oh sure ok"

"Give me a few minutes"

"Please take your time"

 "Okay cool"

"Bye"—shit. I hung up, this nigga was with his girl, I knew it, he has a girl, oh man I'm gonna die why did I call, I knew better, a nigga that fine had to have a girl. I tossed my phone on my couch and sat next to it.

"Ring, ring, ring" it was him.

"Hello"

"Hello Tiffany, sorry about that baby girl I just got home and had to change clothes didn't want to be rude and have you hold on"

"Oh, I understand trust me, anyway how was your day?"

"Pretty interesting so far"

"Oh okay well I'd like to hear about it."

"You know what love, I'd rather hear about yours." I sensed he was avoiding the question so I left it alone.

I didn't tell him the truth—that I thought about him all day, that I couldn't concentrate, that I skipped school, that my body was calling him. Instead I started telling him about my boring job, about how my boss didn't think I knew he watches me and other things. He made me feel comfortable. Thugga's conversation surprised me, he knew something about everything so we were able to talk about politics, sports, fashion, Obama, the earth changing, the disaster in Haiti and finally I asked him if he had anyone in his life. His answer surprised me

"Nobody special, I enjoy having friend's so I fuck with a lot of bitches. I got one that rides out for me better than anyone else so I keep her close, I don't disrespect her and bring other bitches around, she knows but she plays her position." Now usually this would be the part where I hung up, but he kept it real where the average nigga wouldn't so I aint trip, my plan was to make him mine anyway. I asked him what he did for a living, when he told me that wasn't a conversation for the phone that's when I knew he sold drugs.

I found myself breaking all my rules for Thugga. If you can't tell by now I'm a good girl, that's how my mom raised me. I didn't date drug dealers but shit, I do now. Thugga would be the only other man I had since Jermaine. Jermaine was my first everything but I was planning on making Thugga my second no matter what it took.

# Chapter 13

*Thugga*

I couldn't believe how easy and gullible this fine ass bitch was. I could tell Tiffany was green to certain shit. She told me about some lame ass nigga she use to fuck with and she aint never fuck with anyone else, I knew then when I got the pussy she was gonna be mine.

I told her about Kiki and my other bitches and she went for it. That's when I decided to mold her and keep her by my side; after all she's bad, and I love the fact that she can hold a conversation. With Kiki all I can talk about is the streets.

"So Thugga, when am I gonna get to see you again?" Tiffany asked.

"Well, let me see what I got poppin tomorrow and we'll take it from there, but yo! I just got in and I gotta take care of something."

"Please don't let little old me stop you." I laughed I knew Tiffany was trying to be cute and it worked.

"Aight lil' mama—one."

"Bye." I would have liked to finish talking to baby girl but I had three large garbage bags in front of me that needed attention. My mind ran across this nigga Black for a minute. Damn, my lil' nigga, why did he have to do that cruddy shit? He should be here with me counting this money. When I was a kid a nigga killed my popps for bread and I swore I would never let anyone play with mine. If my father would have protected his money better he'd be here now.

I had to shake that thought off no need in crying about it now. I got up, got the money counting machine, a blunt and did my thing. I loved to hear the steady click clack of the machine. As I counted up the birds I realized Paco got away, I only found 50 keys. That nigga was a king pin, he could clean his teeth with 50 keys but it's all good I'm 50 keys richer and he had five hundred thousand dollars in cash that was now mine.

I couldn't believe it. Do you know how long it took the average street nigga to make five hundred thousand dollars? I also knew how fast it could be spent so I decided to hide this shit. I had 150 thousand of my own, 100 from God's Son, another 50 for escape money just in case a nigga had to run and couldn't get back to my stash and I had 45 thousand in drugs before the 50 keys I just got off Paco, so I had enough to flip and spend without touching the five hundred thousand. I was good the way I figured it. If I make this bread work for me instead of becoming a slave to it, I'll be able to retire in know time. I gotta pick up the ten keys Ruby Red got for me and hit the streets, but for now I gotta get these 50 keys out of my crib. "Ring" Ruby Red's phone rang once and went straight to voice mail, that was her way of telling me she was with Kiki so watch what I say when I call her.

"Ring, ring, ring"

"Hey big homie what it look like?"

"Its lookin good ova here, I got some of that powdered milk for the baby got a good price on it she'll never go hungry again can you pick them up today?"

"Sure and thanks, she was starving. Hold up here's your wife."

"Hey daddy I miss you."

"I miss you to honey buns, what ya'll doing?"

"Shoppin"

"Well I got good news."

"I heard. You know this bitch deaf so her phone on extra loud, congratulations"

"Thank you"

"How's Black and Paco?"

"Oh they both had headaches and went home"

"I'll be home soon daddy"

"Yeah yeah"

"Click." Now just in case you haven't figured it out, this whole conversation was in codes.

# Chapter 14

*Kiki and Ruby Red*

"Girl imma have some fun tonight."

"I hear that Kiki, you really love him don't you?"

"Man, love aint the word Ruby, he's my everything, I don't know what I would do without that nigga. Word up, you might as well fuck around and just shoot me if he left me, Thugga aint no real 'in love' type nigga but he does things to show me he cares you know what I mean?"

"Nah bitch, I aint in your shit like that, what he do?"

"Well, he cares about me. He gets me what I want no matter what it is, he aint never play me for no bitch, and never hit me , and you know how niggas get they'll beat a bitch quick."

"Kiki you said it so I'm gonna ask, if he aint no 'in love' type nigga, you sure you got a future with this him?"

93

"Well, you been my best friend for as long as I can remember so imma just tell you the truth. I really don't know, but look like this, bitches want Thugga, and I'm pretty sure he fucks up sometime and gets his dick wet, but he aint never bring one of his bitches in my face, and he always comes home at night. Besides, that man got some powerful dick I mean even if he did me wrong I'd still never leave him.

'Who you telling' I wanted to tell Kiki, shit, when he fucks me I think I'm losing my fucking mind sometime. It's like he don't just fuck, but more like he's putting his all into it, the stress of the streets, his father's death, his feelings for you, his life, everything. You can feel his struggle, his power, his drive and determination in every stroke. Let's just be real Thugga's that nigga.

Do I feel bad about it? Fuck yeah I do. Kiki's my best friend and has been for a long time. We use to boost as kids, as we got older we started robbing people at gun point on the street, then going out of town for niggas, then robbing the nigga's we use to go out of town for til one day a hustler we robbed named Inch found out where I lived and ran up in my crib. He tied me up, beat me, and raped me for six hours.  Kiki came looking for me, as Inch got off me and put his dick away Kiki shot him in the back. The first nigga she ever killed, but sure won't be the last.

Now Ruby Red is my best friend, we been through it all and I love her to death but there's just something in my body that tells me she fucked Thugga before. The way she looks at him, sometimes she makes funny faces at things he says, and I'm not usually around when she's cooking his coke. He taught her well but for some reason he always wanna watch her. 'She might steal a few grams and blame it on cooking losses' he says. Now Thugga know stealing from him is like stealing from me, and the bitch just aint gonna do me like that. Then she don't think I know whenever I'm around and he calls her she sends him to voicemail before she answer's. A definite sign something is going on. Now I don't wanna be known as the jealous crazy girlfriend so before I jump out there and kill this bitch, I'll get proof first.

"Hey girl, let's go in this Gucci store really fast" I told Ruby. "Shit! Look at these Gucci shoes, I gotta find a dress to match this shit."

"Kiki? Kiki! Is that you?" When I turned around I couldn't believe it, it was my old friend from back in the day Tina. The first thing I remembered is she used to fight a lot. She wasn't much of a gun clapper but she'd knock a bitch out and since I was about to put a team together and bump this weed off I could put her down.

"Hey girl give me a hug what's poppin bitch!!!!! What you been up to?"

"Shit girl just trying to survive out here you hear me, niggas getting tight with the money tho, this recession fucking it up for the hustlers too. I see you doing your thing tho, I was walking by and seen you all up in this Gucci store."

"Nah, I'm doing alright I guess, getting by. Yo! This my homegirl Ruby Red–Ruby this is Tina. Look, take my number I'm pretty sure I could help you out."

# Chapter 15

*Thugga and Tiffany*

I looked over at Tiffany and decided—fuck it, we been together all day and I aint want it to end. I had to go see these niggas...so I did something I've never done with any other woman other than Kiki. I took Tiff on my pick up run.

"Yo! Tiff I gotta go take care of some shit. I'll bring you with me under one condition"

"Sure what's that?"

"You never tell anyone the things you see me do."

"Thugga you aint never gotta worry about me."

I took her through Boston Rd. We started on Wilson Ave. and worked our way up to Fish Ave, Seymore, Fenton, and Corsa Ave, all the while collecting money.

I thought to myself 'shit, this nigga is really getting it, he just picked up more money then I'll make all year.' But I aint say nothing, never even questioned him about what was going on.

97

He noticed it and loved it. At least he know I aint nosey, the average bitch woulda had a million questions.

"You ok ma?"

"Yep" Tiffany shook her head, "just enjoying you" she said with a smile. I decided to go holla at niggas who hustled in the area first, then hit niggas on the other side of the Bronx, then I'll hit Harlem, Brooklyn and Queens. First spot I went to was Edenwald to holla at my man Bird. I pulled up in front of the building he hustled in front of. He was usually out there watching his workers, and sure enough he was out there. I pulled the Maserati up to the curve, I seen bird jump off the bench he was on and go under his shirt, I totally forgot I had dark tints on this bitch so I jumped up before he started letting off.

"Shit my nigga what you trying to do get me a murder beef?"

"Boy you pull a gun on me I'll kill your family" I said half joking, half serious.

"What brought you over here?" He asked giving me a pound and hug.

"Looking for you, I'll make this short and sweet—I got birds—you my nigga, so I'll give it to you for twenty five a bird"

"Shit say no more that's less than I'm paying now, imma need five a week can you handle that?"

"Call me when you ready." I aint even answer his dumb question. I aint come holla at this nigga and couldn't fill orders, fuck wrong with this nigga. We made it to Gunhill Rd. I had to go holla at my nigga K-Diamonds, he said he was with me and put in an order for seven bricks and he needed them for tomorrow. I hit Bronx River, Boston Secor, the Valley, Coop city, Castle Hill and finally Soundview. Soundview use to be run by Pistol Pete, one of the Bronx most notorious gangstas. The dude had bodies all over the place and the Feds finally put their hands on him. The homie was sentence to four life sentences so I went to see Mack 11. "I'll be back" I told tiffany and jumped out headed to the horse shoe were I found Mack.

"Mack what's poppin?"

"That five. What's shaken tho?"

"A whole lot, I got brick's now you dig"

"Good fuckin look, two days ago my fuckin connect, a nigga named Paco got his noodles blown all over the place; ever heard of him?"

"Nah can't say I have" (how funny was that).

"Fuck it, but look, I need ten birds a week, we good?"

"Got you my nigga, but I'm charging." Mack cut me off before I could tell him my price.

"If I gotta ask I can't afford it homie feel me!"

"Aight. One."

"One" That just put me where I needed to be. That put me close to eight hundred thousand a week. LET'S GET IT.

Later on that night I found myself in a hotel room with Thuggas dick in my mouth. He nutted in my mouth and I know niggas like when you swallow it, but I couldn't. I never did it before and was scared I might throw up so I grabbed the nearest garbage and spit it out. Before that, Thugga had used his hands to brush my hair out my face, he then kissed me softly at first, then passionately. Thugga took me that night, took me to a place I never knew my body could go, it was like…like…it was like the sweetest thing my body has ever known. It was exciting, explosive, chilling, romantic, it was magic. Ever since then we were inseparable, he took me everywhere. Apple Bees, City Island, and Carolines on Broadway in Manhattan. As Chris Rock told his jokes I watched Thugga laugh, he's so handsome. I think I'm falling in love.

Get Right

A Novel by B.R.

Coming Soon.

# Chapter 16

*Kiki*

"Ring, ring, ring"

This bitch was making me sick. Thugga was sleep beside me, we had celebrated our new position and got drunk and fucked all night. His phone been vibrating and I couldn't help but look. Some bitch named Tiffany has been calling him all morning. Some bitches get some good dick and don't know how the fuck to act.

"Yo! Yo! Get the fuck up man, your bitch is calling you."

"What?" Thugga said picking up his phone, as he seen who it was he turned it off. He'd never done that before, he usually answers and barks on a bitch, 'I'm with my girl you buggin' or 'yo! Im with wifey, you aint got no idea what you doing she'll find you and kill you'. I'm a real bitch and as long as Thugga don't play me I aint gotta get jealous and kill them both.

"So you must like her huh?"

"What you talking bout?"

"Tiffany nigga, Tiffany."

"She cool peoples."

"Cool people huh! You slippin Thugga, you spending too much time with this hoe, what, you think I aint noticed. I'm telling you if this bitch come knocking at this door talking bout she pregnant nigga imma kill you, her, and that mother fucking baby." Thugga took a deep breath and got out the bed never even looking at me. "You trippin my nigga I promise I'll do it."

"Didn't you say you holding a meeting today with them hoes you bout to put on your block?"

"Yeah."

"Well focus on that, what hotel ya'll going to?"

"The Motor Inn on Boston Rd."

"You need me there?" he asked me coming back in the room.

"You can make your presents be known if you want. Our conversation aint finished tho, we need to talk later." I was kind of hurt the way he brushed this whole Tiffany thing off but I decided to give it a month. If she was still around I was just gonna shoot that bitch and that would solve that. But no I had to go

handle my business. I got dressed for my
meeting, I couldn't wait.

"What up ladies?" I had the hotel room full with
my soldiers. Ruby Red, Crystal the bitch who
use to fuck with Black, my childhood friend
Diamond and my home girl Tina. I had seen
her in the mall the other day and she told me
she was doing bad and needed some help so
imma put her on.

"We all know why we here so let's get down to
business. I got pounds and I got blocks you dig.
Ya'll know Ruby Red, that's my lieutenant, ya'll
gonna deal directly through her and she'll deal
with me you dig. It's like this—Chrystal,
Diamond, and Tina can become their own
bosses but ya'll gotta share one block. I don't
want no arguments, no fights, no nothing bout
this shit. If I hear ya'll acting up and fighting
over money imma replace all you bitches.
There's enough bread out here for everybody.
You wit me so far?"

"Yeah we wit you" Diamond answered.
Diamond was one of them mullato bitches, half
black half white, blue eyes a white girl shape
but black girl ass. She had jet black hair so
pretty you would think it was fake. She had did
time for stabbing her best friend but wasn't
charged with murder. They hit her with

manslaughter seeing how it was self defense. Her friend was charging at her with a broken bottle.

"For ya'll that aint hustled before, be on point for these few thing's", Kiki continued "the stick up kids cause if you aint got my money imma kill you. With that said imma give you your first pound on consignment" as Kiki spoke Ruby Red tossed them a pound a piece.

"That's gonna cost you $3,000 a piece now that's a good price in New York for some piff any questions?"

"Nah!" Crystal said.

"Crystal you know the hood good show Tina around.  Show her good stash spots and places she can run and hide from the police.

"Knock, knock, knock," as Kiki heard a knock at the hotel door she reached in her waist pulling her 38. revolver. "Oh one of you bitches set me up?" Kiki ran to the door looking out the peephole before putting her gun away and opening the door.

"Hi daddy."

# Chapter 17

*Tina*

I couldn't believe my mother fucking eyes, my knee's got week my mouth got dry, my heart skipped a beat and my pussy got wet. Kiki opened the hotel door and gave someone a hug, when she let him in I seen the most delicious man I've ever seen in my whole life, and right then and there I decided I gotta have him. "Hey baby let me introduce you to the girls. You know Chrystal, this is my friend Diamond and this is my friend Tina, we go way back. Tina, Diamond this is my boo Thugga!" I couldn't believe my ears Thugga! Not my homie Tiffany's Thugga!

"Hi Thugga" I said standing up and shaking his hand. I noticed he was looking me straight in my eyes kinda flirting. 'This nigga is no fucking good' I thought to myself, but he was sexy in a rugged way none the less. Anyway, later on that night Thugga ended up fucking the shit out of me. For the first time in my life someone fucked not only my body but also my mind, it was unbelievable.

"Oh my god, I can't believe I did this to my best friend."

"Just Breath easy Shorty, she won't find out."

"That's not the point, she's my best friend."

After the meeting in the hotel I told Kiki I would catch a cab. As I waited in the front Thugga drove up to me in a Bentley and asked me if I needed a ride. The next thing I know we were in my house going at it like wild animals.

"Look Tina, calm down, I understand Tiffany's your friend, I mean shit she's my woman, I'm just as sorry this happened as you are but there's certain things you just can't fight sweetheart, like chemistry." I laid on his chest as he spoke. "We can continue to do our thing and if at any point you change your mind, you can let me know. But as long as you with me I promise no harm will ever come to you."

"Okay."

"You'll never need for nothing and I'll always fulfill your sexual fantasies." I smiled when he said that and kissed his strong, manly chest. "But you know I fuck with Tiff and KiKi as long as you don't disrespect them we good."

"Okay."

"Imma give Kiki a few guns tonight and tell her to keep them here, that will be my excuse to come in and out of here as I please okay?"

"Okay" he had me right there, I was officially a dirt bag.

Visit Omygahshproductions.com

For music, flyers, internet designs and more.

# Chapter 18

*Tiffany 1 year later*

A lot has changed in the last year. Me and Tina aint really tight no more, she started getting money with a group of bitches and it's like she aint got time for me no more. As for Thugga, he got me a new spot in Manhattan; he stays there with me every now and then but won't live there with me because he still deals with Kiki. Don't judge me, shit! I know I shouldn't be sharing my man, but if you knew Thugga you would share him too; especially once you found out what type of nigga he is. How gentle and loving he could be, and he told me he loves me the other day which is big because to my understanding he never told a chick he loves her. I was the first which makes me special. But he'll leave Kiki alone soon, he hasn't said it, but I know, especially since I'm pregnant— yep! Me and Thugga are gonna be parents. I'm six months to be exact. We're having a baby girl...isn't that crazy, a baby girl. I'm gonna name her Asia and since Thugga made me quit my job, I'm gonna have all the time in the world to spend with her, to see her first smile, laugh, her first step. I'll be able to share her special moments with her teach her how to be a lady, be there for her first boyfriend and first heart break. I'm gonna have a family ya'll, a family.

"Where you headed Tiff"

"To the grocery, store you coming?"

"Nah!"

"Come on Thugga you aint right"

"Shit we got a house full of food, you're the one that wanna pile food upon food"

"I'm pregnant you jerk" I said picking a pillow off the couch where he was sitting and tossed it at him. "You gonna let me wobble my ass in the supermarket by myself?"

"Tiff I gotta finish counting this money" he said getting up and kissing me on the forehead.

"Money, money, money that's all you can think about"

"Shit, you don't say nothing when you want that mother fucker or  when we bought your mom that house in Queens or how about this three hundred thousand dollar condo I bought so you wouldn't have to worry about a place to live ever again" I pushed him on the couch.

"Okay asshole, I get it. Well gimme money now, time to feed *our* baby" I said rubbing my stomach with my right hand and holding out my left hand as Thugga shook his head, and instead of going into the pile on the table he went in his pocket and tossed me a knot.

"Yo don't forget to get me a pizza kit, you know I like making my pizzas from scratch"

"Anything else thy king" I said sarcastically.

"Yeah, and one of them big booty strippa bitches from the point"

"Sure, and after your done I'll kill you both"

"Oh! Jealousy becomes you"

"Fuck off I'll be back soon"

"Okay love you" only if he knew how good that felt to hear that.

"Love you too" I left the condo and headed to the parking garage. The attendant brought my S.U.V. Thugga had bought me one of those new B.M.W. X6, he said I was fat and my belly needed the room. I hate him sometimes, but he also got me a Benz. I got in the X6 and pulled off, it was nice outside sunny but not hot. I reached for a tissue to blow my nose. Ever since I got pregnant my nose ran a lot, I found the box of tissues in the passenger seat. I stopped at the light and looked in the rear view mirror. "Oh shit there it is again." I picked up the phone and called Thugga.

"Yo"

"Baby, that blue BMW is following me again"

"Oh God Tiff, will you get a grip, you and this blue BMW is driving me crazy. You been seeing this shit for months if I let you tell it. Baby aint nobody gonna use no *bright blue BMW* to follow you, we in Manhattan for God sakes; you know how many BMWs is out here?

"Baby I'm telling you it's the same one."

"Then turn around and come home, okay"

"Okay" I didn't argue with him, I didn't tell him to come get me—I should have, but I knew he thought I was buggin. I made a right at the light all the time keeping my eyes on the rear view mirror, the beamer turned with me. "Oh god please let me get home safe." I looked up to make sure the light was still green so I wouldn't have to stop. I just wanted to get the fuck home. Then I felt the SUV slide to the right, this mother fucker hit my car. "Hey, what the fuck you doing asshole?" I yelled out the window, my heart pumping, I was scared I picked up the phone to call Thugga but it hit me again and dropped the phone on the floor. I looked around for a cop, all the fucking police in New York City and I couldn't find one. I rubbed my stomach and told lil' Asia it was ok, she's scared, I know it. And the last thing I remember is the SUV spinning out of control...me screaming...then a crash.

Follow us at Twitter.com/@brthewriter

# Chapter 19

*Thugga*

A lot has changed in the last year, me and Tina got tight. I like the lil' bitch but she can't be more than a friend. I mean she jumps off too easy, she gave me threesomes and some more shit. I love a freak, but cant wife one.

Me and Kiki we fine, she stop bothering me about Tiffany so I learned to cover it up better. She's my bottom bitch, the one that was there from the beginning so she don't deserve no blatant disrespect. Her weed spot is doing five thousand a day and ten thousand on the weekend so she good. She balls a little too much but she'll never go broke, my baby knows I got her.

As for me and Ruby Red, she couldn't take the fact I wouldn't wife her so she stop fucking with me all together and started grinding with Kiki. I don't really give a fuck tho, I get more pussy then a lil' bit.

And my wifey—she pregnant. Yeah ya'll imma have me a lil' female Thugga. I never thought

I'd see the day, but Tiff took me by surprise. I always fuck with gangsta bitches and the difference in Tiff made me fall in love with her. She was everything a nigga could want minus that killer instinct. I love her...I really do, and she's having my daughter Asia. It couldn't come at a better time. I had the streets on smash. My new connect's name is Spyder. He from Brooklyn, but I met him years back in the Bronx. He had a few blocks on smash until he bumped into a nigga named Get Right from my hood. Get Right's an animal and forced Spyder into hiding for a while but that aint stop nothing, his girl Lala  is handling business for him.

"Ring, ring, ring"

"Yo!"

"Baby that blue B.M.W. is following me again"

"Oh God Tiff will you get a grip, you and this blue B.M.W. is driving me crazy. You been seeing this shit for a month if I let you tell it. Baby, aint nobody gonna use no *bright ass blue B.M.W* to follow you. We in Manhattan for god's sake you know how many B.M.W.'s is out here?"

"Baby I'm telling you it's the same one"

"Then just turn around and come back home okay."

"Okay"

I aint feel like going to get her. Ever since she got pregnant she been bugging. Her latest thing was people are following her, there's been times I've run out the house, gun in hand and seen no one, but not today. I just collected some money from Dollar, Grav, and Hussien and had to count it. My plan worked down to the tee, I don't need for shit and neither does anyone around me. We good and thing's can only get better from here.

Visit us at www.brthewriter.com

# Chapter 20

*KiKi*

A lot has changed in the last year. Thugga thinks I only make $5,000 a day off every bitch I got working for me. I can tell him whatever I want because he aint in my business like that. As for me and Thugga—we good, shit is still the way it's always been between us except for when he has to run off to that slut bitch Tiffany's. I knew about her for a while, but one day Tina came to me and told me Tiffany is her best friend and hoped it wouldn't get in the way of our business relationship. But it will, so what I did was give her a cheaper price to snoop around for me. The last time she spoke to Tiffany she said she was pregnant. Girl I tell you I had to take a vacation without Thugga, there was no way I could let him see me in the state of mind I was in. I went to the Poconos, rented a hotel and cried, broke everything in the room and lost ten pounds from the lack of eating. When I got a grip of myself I knew what I had to do--niggas gotta die. I had to keep my word to myself. Well not all of it anyway I could never kill Thugga. After all he's done, he's still my boo and I want him back—but Tiffany, yeah that bitch gone. That's what brings me here in this blue B.M.W. driving behind Tiffany, all kinds of emotions coming out. My eyes tearing, screaming like a mad woman about to kill her, I rammed that nigga stealing bitch with my car as I watched her on the phone, probably talking to my man. Her car didn't spin out of control the way I wanted it to so I hit it again a little harder this time, she dropped her phone I could see her panicking and looking around for help—I chuckled. I wonder whose life this bitch thought she was playing with? I hit her again, this time her precious little S.U.V. spun out of control and hit a pole, fuck your life bitch!

# Chapter 21

*Tina*

I just got a call from Thugga, someone ran Tiffany's car off the road and she is in Jacoby hospital. As soon as he told me I knew it was Kiki, and it was all my fault. My god, what have I done, how could I have betrayed my sister just for the love of money. I let Kiki talk me in to snooping on her just to get a cheaper price on a few pounds. After I told her that Tiffany was pregnant I fell back, I didn't want anything to happen to that poor innocent baby.

My next thought was if Thugga found out I had anything to do with his baby being in the hospital he would kill me. Tears formed in my eyes as I sped down the street running all the lights. "Oh tiffany please be okay" how could Kiki be so heartless? I've been calling her; I hate myself, this isn't her fault it's mine for being so fuckin greedy.

I found a parking spot and ran to the front desk, I gave them Tiffany's name and they told me her room. That must mean she's okay, she isn't in operation, she's in a room, she's resting. I got in the elevator and said a silent prayer, the door opened, fifth floor, this is it. I came out the elevator and my mouth dropped to the fourth floor.

My heart dropped, and I felt faint. I couldn't believe what I was seeing, Thugga was on the floor crying, Dollar over him trying to hold him up, it was like a movie. I went deaf for a second Grav grabbed my arm, he was saying something, his lips were moving but I couldn't hear anything. When I tuned back in he was saying "Bitch do you here me?", I nodded yes, "Tiff's okay but Asia's dead."

# Chapter 22

*Thugga*

After Asia died things changed between me and Tiffany. It's like, I still love her but I can't stand to be around her. I was going through this thing, I blamed her for what happened to my daughter, my precious lil' girl, my Asia. I told that stupid lil' bitch she didn't need to go out, that we had lots of food in the house, but she wouldn't listen and I needed someone to take my rage and anger out on. I watched Tiffany as she lay there in the bed, she looked like an angel as she slept.

"Smack!!!"

"Get the fuck up you no good bitch"

"Thugga please"

"Please what, all you do is sleep all day, look at this place, there's clothes everywhere, and dirty dishes in the fucking sink."

"I'm sorry" I smacked her again only harder this time.

"Smack!!!"

125

"Shut up bitch and stop crying, you're always sorry, you aint good for shit, get the fuck up bitch." Tiffany jumped out of bed stumbling to the ground. I went to help her up, but kicked her instead; blood trickled down her top lip onto her chin.

"Thugga, why are you doing this to me?" she asked holding her hands in her face as defense. I bent over and smacked Tiffany again with the back of my hand "smack" Tiffany started to cry and tremble just wishing it would stop "no good bitch" I said leaving the room, looking back shaking my head at Tiffany in disgust as she curled up in the corner like a baby in her mother's womb. Like my daughter.

"Oh God please let this stop, I can't take this anymore" Tiff cries, tears running down her face mixing in with the blood from her lips "please God let this stop, I can't take this anymore."

# Chapter 23

*Thugga*

After I left the house I went straight home to Kiki. I still have some stress I wanted to take out on somebody so as soon as I walked through the door I grabbed her by her hair put my tongue down her throat and squeezed her ass. I took Kiki in that room and fucked the shit out of her, and I mean that hair pulling, ass smacking, deep thrusting fuck. Kiki screamed so loud I'm surprised no one called the police. I laid there with Kiki on my chest wondering what to do. I couldn't go on like this beating Tiffany and hurting Kiki the way I do, you know being unfaithful and all, if you ask me she's become my side chick. I never meant for it to happen that way, Kiki's a faithful rider. I looked down at her and kissed her forehead, her phone vibrating on the nightstand caught my attention. When she didn't answer her phone, my phone rang, that's when I knew whatever it was it was important.

"Hello"

"Hey Thugga this is Chrystal"

"Yeah what's good with you?"

"Are you around? I need to talk to you"

"Yeah but I'm busy right now"

"I think you'll really want to hear what I gotta tell you yo!"

"Aight I'm at Kiki's, come up." I hung up the phone and woke Kiki "lil' mama get up."

"Why? I'm resting baby."

"You need to get dressed Chrystal's coming over, said she got something she gotta tell me."

"Okay." I watched as Kiki jumped up to grab a quick shower, she really did have a spectacular body. I've still yet to see a shape as fine as hers and don't think I ever will. When she came out I watched as she put lotion on, got dressed, put on her high heels and took a look at herself in the mirror. 'Beautiful' I thought to myself, imma have to put some serious thought into who I want to be with. If I choose Tiffany there's no way I can remain faithful to her. Not with the young stallion I got standing in front of me. "Ding dong" the door bell ringing broke my train of thought, but I made a mental note to myself to put some serious thought into my decision. I put my pants and Tims on, no shirt and went to the door.

"Nasty ass you aint gonna get in the shower?" Kiki asked

"Nah I want the scent of your pussy all over my balls all day."

"Nasty, now that's the real definition of a dirty dick nigga." I laughed at KiKi's joke before looking through the peephole and seeing Crystal standing out their alone.

"Crystal what's poppin kid?"

"A lot" Crystal said walking by me so fast you would think she was being followed.

"Yo, Crystal you okay baby? You're shaking what's wrong?" Kiki asked as she held on to Chrystal's hand, I could see how concerned Kiki was for her friend by the look on her face. She walked Chrystal over to the couch, I took a seat next to her asking what was wrong knowing in my stomach that I wasn't gonna like the answer. Chrystal turned around to face me, straight in my eyes.

"You know my home girl Sharell from Harlem? The one I'm always with, well she started fucking with Dollar a few months back. She brought that nigga to Harlem and niggas around the way say he out their bragging bout setting some nigga up in the Bronx, said he use to steal money from some big time hustler and blamed it on dude in order to get him out the way and get more money. The part that really fucked me up is he said he did it so smooth that he aint even have to pull the trigger, he made it that the big time nigga did it. Before I jumped to any conclusions I had Sharell pick Dollar's brain...Thugga he set you up to kill Black."

# Chapter 24

*The War*

I couldn't believe Thugga's reaction to what Crystal just told us. He cried—not a 'boo-hoo' cry but a man's cry, you know a tear or two rolling down his face, and then I remembered it was him that pulled the trigger that killed Black.

I tried to comfort him but he wasn't having it, all he wanted was revenge for Black's unjustified death, and said he needed help from me and the girls. He wanted things to end, and it would end tonight. The plan was for me to knock off Hussein, Diamond would handle Grav, and Thugga would take care of Dollar himself. We would all meet up later tonight just in case we needed alibis we can say we were with each other. Hussein was renting the basement of a private house in Staten Island so I caught the fairy out there, then I caught a cab. Of course I had my clean up bag with me so I reached inside and took out my ski mask and wrapped it around my hand and broke the  window  to his bedroom and let myself in.

This stupid ass nigga had all types of drugs and money in there with no type of alarm, not even a fucking dog. He deserves for a nigga to rob him, which is exactly what I was gonna make this look like so I trashed the place, took the money, jewelry, and his drugs, that's when I heard the soft ass nigga putting his key in the door. I took my position right behind it "what the fuck? Oh man you gotta be fucking kidding me some body rob my fucking crib" Hussein never seen me coming as I hit him in the back of the head with my desert eagle. I swung the door shut as he hit the floor. I kicked him in the side hard enough to break his ribs, he aint make no noise so I knew he was knocked out. I went to my clean up bag for some rope and tied Hussein up like a pig, hands to ankles and dragged him to his bed. Once I had him on it facing me I put some smelling salt under his noise.

"Oh! What the fuck" Hussein opened his eyes and fixed them on me, he stared as if he seen a ghost.

"Hi Hussein!" in a voice that sounded deranged even to me, but I was mad, hurt, confused and ready to draw blood. They killed my friend, my lil' brother someone I helped raise, and for what...jealousy.

"KiKi what's good yo!? What the fuck you doing dog?"

"Giving you what you deserve, how could you Hussein?" I asked pacing back and forth forcing Hussein to keep his eyes on me. "How could you do Black like that?"

"Kiki, that wasn't even me son, word up! Real rap Kiki, but that nigga *Dollar*, dog he hated Black, he wanted his position, he said Black had all the things he couldn't have, all the bitches, cars, clothes, blocks, respect, everything; and he wanted him dead. Kiki you gotta believe me, you know me better than that, I wouldn't do no shit like that it wasn't me homie it was Dollar!"

"And you went right along with it, see I was gonna make this fast, you know shoot you in your head and shit but because you lied imma make this interesting."

KITTY KAT CREW

A Novel by B.R.

Coming soon

# Chapter 25

*Diamond*

When Kiki called me and asked me to help put in some work I was honored. I guess about the fact that she knew I was strong enough to put this type of work in, plus it showed she trusted me. I put my own version of her clean up bag together. Mine consist of masking tape, a razor, gun, mask, gloves and that salt people throw on the floor after it snows. It was time to get it, and I was ready and anxious, so anxious I could taste Grav's blood in my mouth. I swear today Grav met a gangsta.

"Diamond, if you don't cut this tape off me bitch imma kill you."

"I aint gonna be the one to die today Grav."

"What the fuck you talking bout bitch."

"Your mother."

I had told Grav I was gonna give him some pussy, and I'm a bad bitch, there was no way he was gonna turn me down. So just like a nigga he took me straight to his whole in the wall he called an apartment. This ol' small time hustling ass nigga; and to top it off this nigga had the nerve to pull out a bottle of Rose but not the Don P shit, but the Moet shit. So I drunk the nigga liquor got naked and let the nigga eat my pussy. Shit, he was so good at it I almost changed my mind about killing the nigga. That's when he started telling me how bad I am, how sexy my body is, how my pussy taste good, blah blah, you know the average shit when a nigga got a bad bitch like me in the bed—lame. If he had kept his mouth shut instead of sweating me like everybody the fuck else I probably would have gave him some before he died, but he sounded way too thirst so I changed my mind and told him how freaky I was feeling and wanted to tie him up.  Of course, he went along with that.

"You fucking with the wrong nigga home girl."

"Your name Grav" I laughed "yeah, you the right pussy nigga I was looking for."

"Pussy huh! Okay home girl, the money's in the safe under the bed. The combo 2323, take the money and get the fuck out my house."

"Oh good looking my nigga, I'll take that but that aint what I came for, enough talking time to get to work." I taped Grav mouth shut and pulled my razor out the clean up bag and watched as Grav eyes grew wide like he just took a hit of some coke. The first time I swung the razor it connected with his face blood flew all over the place, I could see Grav close his eyes in pain. I hurt him, but little did he know this was only the beginning.

"umm, ummmmm …."

"What? Are you saying something Grav? Oh that's right I can't hear you, you got tape on your mouth. I swung the razor again this time cutting him from his eye to his mouth, it cut the tape so I heard him yell.

"Aaaaaah!"

"Oh shit, my bad homie, that was sloppy work."

"Please! Please!" I taped his mouth shut ignoring his plead, he was crying now, face full of blood and eyes full of fear, he noticed me watching and closed his eyes.

"Oh no homeboy, you're gonna watch this." I bent down, and like a surgeon handy with a knife, I cut away both Grav's eye lids. I had to laugh, it was bloody but he looked like one of them skeletons; you know how their eyes just look open all the time. I reached in my clean up bag and pulled out the bag of salt "I know this might hurt a little bit but it will all be over soon" I dipped in the bag and poured a handful in Grav's wounds, he yelled the best he could behind the tape, and then he stopped moving "hey no fair" I checked for a pulse; he was still alive, so I guess he was just knocked out. It was hard to tell because his eyes was permanently open. I took the back of my hand and smacked him like the bitch he is. He started wiggling around as if he never passed out "Oh this is hilarious, I wish I had a video camera I would youtube this shit." I figured Grav had suffered enough and slit his throat, leaving him to bleed out.

# Chapter 26

*Thugga's Revenge*

I called Dollar and told him to meet me at his house because I had something important I wanted to talk to him about. I couldn't believe what he'd done, how could he betray me like this? Then I thought about myself and felt disgusted. The fact that I reacted without thinking, Black was my lil' man how can I have not given him the benefit of the doubt. Oh man Dollar's gotta pay.

I've been seeing flashes of Black's face ever since we found out the truth. I kept on picturing the confused look on his face when he seen me pointing my gun at him. My lil' homie wasn't pussy either, the lil' nigga raised that gun and pulled the trigger, and when he realized he was about to die he held it down, no crying, no begging for his life, not even a blink "Fuck Black...forgive me man" I said banging my fist against the steering wheel.

I parked the R8 across the street from Dollar's crib and rolled a blunt out of a back wood while I waited for this crut ball ass nigga Dollar to show up. I got some good piff I got from Fordham road. The shit had me choking and thinking evil, maybe I'll kill him and drop him off on his mother's front door, or leave him at his baby's mother's job, drop his dead body in his son's school playground. No matter what I did he deserved it. A man lost his life out of jealousy—because of him. I put the weed I was smoking out as I seen Dollar's Benz pull up, he was looking in my car but couldn't see in, the tints is dark as shit. He damn near strained his eyes trying to see inside as he approached the car. He stood there for a second as I watched him, he finally knocked on my window, I took my time winding it down, not for added affect but because I was trying to get my emotions under control before I spoke to him. A true gangsta moves with intelligence over emotions, and right now I was more of an emotional wreck. I took a deep breath and let the window down.

"Fuck wrong with you nigga? You look like you just lost your best friend." Dollar's words put a knot in my stomach.

"I did, a few months back remember?" I waited patiently for his reaction, some remorse, anything. But I got nothing instead Dollar looked at me as if he were saying 'what's that about' then shook it off.

"Yeah ok anyway, you said you got to holla at me about something what's good big homie?"

"Yeah this might take a minute let's go inside duke."

"Duke?" Dollar whispered to himself and stepped back as I opened the car door. I followed him to the house, he stuck the key in the door and opened it and without looking back he said "Yo! Why don't we go someplace else and have this talk my baby mom bout to drop my son off."

"Yo! Go in the house lemme holla at you real quick" I said pushing him in the door.

"Why the fuck you pushing me like that?" Dollar must have sensed what time it was cause before I knew it he turned around and punched me in my lip, I stumbled back but shook it off real fast and two pieced that nigga. He hit the floor and I jumped on him with the intentions of beating all the fear of God into this lil' nigga. I rained on him like Katrina, busting his lip, his nose gushed blood like it was broke and his right eye swole up like he been hit with a hammer. With the swiftness, I backed out the knife I've been carrying, flipped

141

it open and drew my hand back. He tried to use his body to throw me off him but his frail frame was no match for my muscular upper body. I swung the knife straight for his throat. He grabbed my wrist with both hands so I used my left hand to help my right, the harder I push the heavier Dollar's breathing. The room was silent, so silent I could swear I heard his heart beating as the knife came closer to his throat. As soon as the tip touched him I smiled "that's right, you ready to die Dollar?" I saw the first speck of blood. "Oh here it comes baby" Dollar started shaking, he let my wrist go and held on to the knife but within seconds, it was over.

# Chapter 27

*Thugga*

After I left Dollar's house I went to me and Kiki's little spot. I jumped in the shower and washed Dollar's blood off of me. As the water hit my back I felt a weight lift off of my shoulders. Black was still gone though, there was no bringing him back but at least I got revenge for his death. I jumped out the shower and got dressed. I'm supposed to meet Kiki and the girls at this club called "The Door" in Manhattan to celebrate Black's life. It was only right we did that today than any other day. I checked myself in the mirror and then called Tiff to let her know I wouldn't be home today. I didn't get an answer so I tried again and just like the first time it rang out. "Fucking bitch." I figured she was mad about the ass whipping I gave her earlier, it's all good. All I had to do was buy the bitch some diamonds and roses later and she'll be okay. Even though Ruby Red don't fuck with me no more I still decided to give her a call and invite her to Black's celebration, after all she was just as close to him as we were. Her cell went straight to voicemail same shit as yesterday when I tried to call her for help with the work we just put in. 'She must not want to talk to anyone' I thought, all good tho.

I pulled the Benz in front of the club. There was mad niggas on line but more bitches then anything and they came out showing off tonight. Legs, breast, toes peeking out at a nigga and dresses so tight you can see pussy prints and mean ass shots. "Damn why Kiki had to be here tonight." I jumped out to holla at the niggas I knew and seen a few chicks I wouldn't mind getting with. I parked my shit in a lot that wasn't too far and as I walked back to the club KIKI text me:

> *'Where u at daddy? U bullshitting this shit is jumpin. That nigga red café jus showd up wit uncle murda I think they might perform'*

I fucks with both red café and uncle murder so I put a little pep in my step hoping not to miss their performance. So I text KIKI back:

> *'Im out frnt. b there in a minit*

I tip the bouncer and skip the line going straight to the ticket booth, paid for my ticket got patted down by a bouncer that was way

144

over weight and walked through the doors as Young Jeezy blared through the speakers "I put on for my city" I sang with the song and seen Kiki in the back reppin for our borrow tossing up the BX sign. I gave her a hug and a kiss and acknowledged the other girls. Damn now all I got is a crew full of woman I thought to myself then remembered they bang harder than a lot of dudes. The D.J. put some old B.I.G. on and the crowd started rocking and singing every line as I ordered my bottles. I noticed the chicks that call themselves the Y.G.Bs. They work for my connect Spyder and they put work in; shoot, cut, stab and kill anyone who gets in their way. I respect them, especially Lala, she runs them bitches with a steal fist, I raised my bottle at them. Baby Blue blew me a kiss, I went to school with her and wanted to fuck her for the longest. I looked at KIKI hoping she aint peep that shit because there woulda been trouble up in this bitch. But I know Baby Blue, she aint really give a fuck when she did it. She bangs with the best of them. My phone rang and the number was blocked. Now I usually don't answer blocked calls but Tina, Tiffany and Ruby Red were all M.I.A. so I decided to answer.

"Hello"

"This is a collect call. This call is from...Tina...please press five to except the call"

"What the fuck" I said pressing five.

"Hello!"

"Yo! Thugga they got me in the 47th prescient somebody told, they ran up in my crib and found all the guns."

"Well why the fuck you calling me?"

"What? Thugga don't fucking play with me. I'll be in court next week but the judge gave me a bail, its ten thousand Dollars I need you to come get me out."

"Yeah aight!" I said hanging up, this bitch stupid if she think imma put my name on the dotted line that got anything to do with some guns. Nobody but me and Kiki knew she had them, if Tina would have kept her mouth shut instead of telling her home girls her business she wouldn't be locked up now. I focused back on Baby Blue and caught her watching me, yeah I was gonna hit that tonight. I lost focus when I heard Kiki yelling over the music, she was on the phone. I knew it was Tina when Kiki shot me that look, Tina must have told her I hung up on her.

"Yo! What type of shit you on" Kiki asked me.

"What you mean?"

"You know what the fuck I'm talking about. My home girl called asking for some help and you hung up on her?"

"Did you tell somebody we put guns in her house?"

"Nah."

"Well me either, that mean Tina was running her fuckin mouth. That's her problem now"

"Your fucked up Thugga. Them is your guns the girl is going to jail for. She aint ask to hold them, you did. You changing on us Thugga and that's crazy, but always remember God don't like ugly and what goes around comes around." I watched as Kiki got the girls and rolled out, fuck them I thought. The champagne was starting to get to me, my dick was getting hard and Baby Blue was still watching me when Kiki left. I was about to make my move when I noticed Baby Blue coming my way.

"What's up Thugga?" she said taking a seat.

"Whats poppin?"

"Come on now, you know aint nothing poppin with me, it's always cracking."

"Oh my bad" I had forgot she was crip, they say what's cracking and bloods say what's poppin. I don't be paying that shit no attention, I only bang for me and my cause no one else's.

"I see your crew of chicken heads finally left."

"Cute" I laughed. "But fuck them what's up with you?" I asked pouring her a drink.

"I been good, but if I was going home with you tonight I would be even better."

"Say no more, you got my number right?"

"Yeah."

"Okay hit me when you ready" I gave Baby Blue a kiss sucking on her bottom lip and getting up to leave. I've waited a long time for that pussy and tonight I was gonna beat that up.

# Chapter 28

*Tina*

I couldn't believe this shit, who the fuck this nigga think he is. I had his fucking guns in my house, guns he asked me to hold and this pussy ass nigga had the nerve to hang up on me. I aint even have to be here, they gave me the opportunity to tell on him and they would let me go, but I aint no fucking rat and I'll never be. It even say's so in the Bible, 'never use your tounge to hurt thy neighbor', so instead I keep my mouth shut and this is what he does—ooooh! Revenge is gonna be so sweet on this pussy ass nigga. I would tell Kiki about us, knowing she would kill that nigga for fucking her close friend, but she would probably kill me too so I decided against it. When Thugga hung up on me I called Kiki, thank God she told me she was on her way to come get me out of this hell hole cause I was ready to get the fuck out of here. There was all types of chicks in here, bitches who just caught murder beefs, some was dressed like they just came off the track, and there was junkies laying on the floor in their own vomit.

"Where's Miss Tina Willams?" I heard a female guard call my name.

"Right here"

"What holding cell are you in?" 'I don't know bitch' I thought to myself, I looked around the cell and finally spotted the number 5 "Im right here, cell five" a slim brown skin chick who looked like she should have been in the projects smoking a blunt came to get me. "My bail finally came through?"

"No, but we got someone who would like to see you, follow me down this hallway to the back room." I wondered what was going on, I seen my lawyer already so who could this be?

"Please take a seat, someone will be in to talk to you soon." I took a seat in what looked to be an interrogation room. A tall white man with black hair that look like it just been colored came into the room. He was dressed in a suit, tie, and some expensive looking shoes. He took a seat in front of me and opened a folder; it was full of pictures. I couldn't see of who, but my guess is I'm about to find out. "How are you Miss Willams, I'm homicide detective John Maclairin" holy shit homicide detective, what the fuck is this about?

"Hello"

"Now let me start by saying you're not in trouble here Ms Williams but all phone calls are monitored here and we have reason to believe that people you've contacted since you've been here know something about the murder and attempt murder of these two gentlemen." He slid the photos to me, and thank God I didn't know either of them. They were both laid out on the floor with what looked to be shots to their heads. I slid it back not wanting to look at that shit any longer.

"Nope never seen them before in my life and I really doubt any of my friends know them."

"Take a good look Ms. Williams" he said sliding the folders back to me. "That's Paco Cartier aka Paco and Tyrone Gibson aka Black" my heart skipped a beat when I heard Black's name. I've never met him but Kiki and Thugga spoke about him often "you see, whoever did this fucked up, Paco's dead but Black is in a coma and when he comes out of it, I'll have all the information I need."

Get Right

A Novel by B.R.

Coming Soon

# Chapter 29

*Thugga*

The sound of my phone ringing woke me up. I reached for it sliding Baby Blue off my chest. We went at it like savages last night; she's so petite I ain't think she could hang with me, but shorty went in. Five rounds of fucking and sucking, I touched every inch of her beautiful body. Her breasts were perfect, lips soft and her pussy was sweet, I even sucked the pretty little bitch's toes word up! Baby Blue called me when she left the club, I went and picked her up and as soon as we got in the room she jumped her 5' 2" frame on me and it was on and poppin in that room for about the next three hours. She put work in, I gotta give it to her, cause besides KIKI no other bitch I'm fucking with put that much work in, not even Tiffany.

As Tiff ran through my mind I made a mental note to call her. I aint heard from her in two days. No matter how mad she's been at me she's never went this long without calling me. I took a look at my phone and noticed I had twenty missed calls. I was sure it was from

Tiffany, but it wasn't it's from Kiki and that wasn't like her to blow my phone up so I called her back.

"Hello! Thugga where you at? Never mind I don't even wanna hear your trifling ass lie to me, but while you been laid up with one of your hoes we was bailing Tina out, Thugga a homicide detective asked her about Paco and Black."

"What!?" I said sitting up in the bed scaring Baby Blue out her sleep. "But she don't know neither one of them" I yelled.

"I know but he said she called someone from the jail that had something to do with it" shit I'm fucked I thought. She only called Kiki and me, and I know they don't think Kiki did it.

"And Thugga, Black's alive."

I couldn't believe what Kiki had just said, it took a moment for it to sink in. I was full of different emotions, my lil' man aint dead, I didn't kill him, I imagined myself going to get him and showing him how far we've come and give him his rightful spot next to me. I couldn't wait to see Black enjoy spending more money than he ever dreamed of making. I bet he'd buy a Benz he loves those shits.

"I called every hospital until I found him he's in Jacobi hospital" Kiki said

"I'll meet you there, I'm on my way."

"Everything okay honey?"

"I don't have time I'll explain everything to you later I promise" I told Baby Blue  as I kissed her on her forehead instead of her lips, she'd been sucking my dick all night I aint wanna know what that smelled like, much less taste like. I slammed the door on my way out running to my car, shirt in hand, I'd been in such a rush I didn't put it on so I threw it on as I got in the car and pulled out the hotel parking lot. My tires screamed as I exited the lot. My heart was racing out of excitement as I dipped in and out of traffic blowing my horn for people to get the fuck out of my way. I threw the car in park and left that shit in front, I aint really give a fuck I needed to see my homie.

"Excuse me miss could you tell me what room Tyrone Gibson is in?"

"Umm sir, those two Gentlemen over there asked to speak to anyone who wanted to see Mr.Gibson" as I looked over there I seen two plain clothed officers coming my way.

"Mr. Clark I'll need you to turn around for me and please place your hands behind your head."

"For what, what did I do "

"Your being arrested for the murder of Paco Cartier and the attempt murder of Tyrone Gibson."

# Chapter 30

*Thugga*

When we got to the 47th precinct I called my lawyer right away. I kept one on hand, I gave him a hundred thousand dollars a while ago, that should be enough to pay for a trial, and we taking this one all the way baby. The way I figured it, Black aint no rat and they aint got no evidence against me.

"Hello, Kevin Allen's office how can I help you?"

"This is Sean Clark can I speak to Mr. Allen please?"

"Hold on sir."

"Hey Mr. Clark how are you?"

"I'm in bad shape Kevin, I'm in the 47th precinct and I need you now!"

"What's the charges?"

"One count of murder and a second count of attempted murder."

"Okay look don't let them question you, if they ask you anything tell them you plead the fifth and won't be answering any questions until the arrival of your attorney, you got it?"

"Yeah and Kevin hurry." When I got off the phone I thought of every excuse to tell them. 'I couldn't have done it I was with KIKI that night', or 'I knew Black but never met Paco sorry!' Whatever I say it had to be believable. My thoughts were broken when I heard the door behind me open; I turned around and was faced with this ugly old faced cracker smiling at me.

"You have no idea how many months I've been on this case, and now I'm in front of the man who master minded it all, I got you Sean I really do."

"I aint got nothing to say till my lawyer get's here."

"Oh that's okay, I'll wait, I've waited months for this moment Sean...or should I say Thugga?" Now that fucked me up, this cracker knew more about me than I thought. I need a cigarette.

"Yo! Can I get a cigarette?"

"You watch too much TV. No you can't have a fucking cigarette."

"Sean what's going on, I told you not to answer any questions till I get here."

"I can assure you sir, I haven't asked him anything. I'm detective O'connor"

"I'm Mr. Clark's attorney, Kevin Allen."

"Mr. Allen, please, have a seat next to your client if you will"

"Thank you, now may I ask you what this is about?"

"Well it turns out that we are charging Mr. Clark with murder and attempted murder."

"What proof do you have detective? Any? I'm pretty sure my client has an alibi."

"That's funny because we have his fingerprints at the scene of the crime, and neighbors that say they saw Mr. Clark leaving the deceased man's home. Anything you would like to tell me Sean?"

"Look I aint kill nobody both Paco and Black are friends of mine why would I do something like that?"

"Look we can do this two ways Sean, and I'd like to see you help yourself, if you tell me what happened I'll ask the D.E.A. to give you life. If you lie to me Sean, they're gonna push for the death penalty. What's it gonna be?"

"Death penalty! Life!" I yelled "talking like that you can go fuck yourself."

"Sean please" my lawyer said.

"Nah man! This nasty pig mother fucker acting like he trying to do me a favor. No matter which one I choose they taking my fucking life from me."

"Good stuff. Hey can I get an officer to take this kid away. You played yourself kid; see you in court Mr. Allen" my lawyer waited until the detective left the room.

"Look Sean, hang on tight, we will see the judge tomorrow and get you a bail and we'll take it from there okay!"

I had to sleep in a raggedy, pissy cell last night. As I was on the bus I thought about Kiki. I knew my boo would be there with the bail money, and I couldn't wait to see her. I had to sit on this fucking bus and listen to these lying ass niggas tell stories about why they were locked up, just a lot of petty shit. Dime sales, niggas hitting their baby mothers and weed possession charges, nothing compared to what I'm facing. The bus pulled up to the court house and we were told to file off the bus one by one and give our names. We were then taken to the back and uncuffed, walked through a metal detector and placed in a cell. Forty of us packed in a space that had only enough room for thirty people. Niggas was aggravated, fights broke out and rival gangs were trying to kill each other. Instead of making room in the cell the cops would just come get the ones who were fighting and put someone else in their spot.

"Sean Clark"

"Yeah!"

"Come to the front of the cell, your attorney wants to see you." They took me to a room with glass in between me and my lawyer "Kevin any good news?"

"Not really Sean. I spoke to the D.A. they got evidence against you Sean"

"What kind of fucking evidence?"

"Your fingerprints on Mr. Cartier's safe, they also have neighbors that said you frequently visited Mr. Cartier. Sean I don't know if you did it but it doesn't look good, we gotta come up with something and we gotta do it fast. Look your next in court, I'll get you bail and get you out of here then we'll find out the best way to get at this thing. You ready?"

"I guess, shit, it's now or never." The judge they gave me was so old I thought he would die right there in front of his desk. As they told us to be seated I looked around and saw no one. No Kiki, no Tina, no Ruby Red, not even Tiffany. The prosecutor pulled my lawyer aside, I couldn't hear them but hoped it was good news until Kevin looked back at me and shook his head. "Shit!" It didn't look good and I could see it written all over Kevin's face.

"Not good Sean."

"What?"

"What the detective didn't tell us was they found your finger prints on one of the guns found at Tina Jackson's house and matched the same prints to the safe, they matched that to your finger prints they took from you on Rikers Island so they know they got the right guy."

"You can talk to your client later Mr. Allen let's get this bail hearing started" the judge said.

"Thank you your honor I move that we give Mr. Clark a reasonable bail, he has no job and no family sir, and it would be hard for him to make a high bail. He has no violence in his past so he can hardly be considered a threat to the community."

"Okay Mr. Allen, I'll keep that in mind. Mr. Pine!" the judge gave the prosecutor a chance to dispute the bail.

"Well your honor, if counsel doesn't consider a man who's being charged for murder ad attempt murder a treat to the community then I don't know what is. Mr. Clark also has an old conviction for possession of crack cocaine with the intent to distribute in 1999 and it's been brought to my attention the defendant has a weapon charge separate from this case your honor. I believe Mr. Clark has the potential to become a flight risk in order to avoid prosecution."

"I would have to say I agree with the prosecution. Bail denied! Next case please."

"Kevin. That's it?"

"There's nothing I can do Sean. Look, let me research your case and I'll be here to see you in a few days. Be strong I got it."

For any questions or concerns email me at
BR@BRTHEWRITER.COM

# Chapter 31

*Thugga*

I couldn't believe this shit. Two mother fucking crackers, who don't know shit about me, just sat there and decided whether the things I done with my life makes me dangerous, but yet they know nothing I've done and never heard of me in their lives. So now I'm back on this bus on my way to Rikers Island, one of the worst of the worst when it comes to state prisons. I aint really give a fuck though, I'm a motherfucking gangsta, and any nigga who tries me will soon find out. I just needed to get to the phone I needed Kiki, I needed Tiffany. We pulled up to the intake section of the Island where we were stripped searched and given identification numbers, that way there was no mistakes about who we were. They sent me to the housing unit. I couldn't do the dorm thing, I needed my privacy. I walked around the unit to make sure none of my enemies from the street was in here. You know how niggas do, they'll fuck around and try to pop on you when you aint looking, or run up in your mother fucking cell when you sleep. I got on line for the phone.

165

As I waited I noticed a few niggas walking by me mean mugging. I'd have to check that out later, niggas got me fucked up. When my turn came up I jumped on the jack calling Tiffany first. I was a little more worried about her than anything, I haven't heard from my honey buns in a few days.

"Hello."

"Yo! Who dis?"

"This is Tiffany's mother Sean."

"Oh, I'm sorry Miss Jones, is Tiffany there?" I asked, wondering why the fuck she was answering Tiffany's phone.

"Yeah Sean, but I have something to talk to you about."

"With all due respect maam, this is important and I really need to talk to her."

"Well so is this Sean. What you and my daughter had is finished Sean."

"What!?"

"You heard me it's over, you've hurt and beat my daughter for way too long. Have I known about it, things would have been over long ago Sean."

"Listen Miss Jones."

"No, you listen Sean. I'm not Tiffany, if I ever hear about you calling her again I will be sure to call the cops and press charges for assault and battery myself."

I couldn't believe this shit. Miss Jones hung up in my fuckin ear. How the fuck could Tiff do this to me. Regardless of how I been acting lately I changed her life for the better. I even bought her mother a house, this is the first bitch I ever loved and this is how she repays me.

"Shit" I had to grab hold of myself. Fuck it, I need a support team and I was about to put one together starting with Ruby Red.

"Ding, ding, ding. The number your trying to reach has been disconnected." I had to laugh. Bitch stop fucking with me, now she can't even pay her fucking phone bill. I hung up and tried Kiki.

"Hello."

"Baby, where are you?" I asked Kiki.

"In the house, what up, why you calling me blocked for?"

"Kiki I'm locked up, they got me."

"Well why you calling me bitch."

"What, hello! Hello?" Kiki lost her motherfucking mind, she hit me with the same shit I told Tina. I really aint got time for this bullshit and tried to call her back.

"A yo!, phone check homie."

"What?" this stupid little 5 foot 7 inch nigga must be on a suicide mission or something. I just reacted without thinking and punched this dude straight in his nose. His eyes watered and nose started to bleed, I took the receiver off the phone and started swinging it hitting duke in the eyes and head. The nigga hit the floor and curled up like some bitch.

"Drop the phone or I'll mace you I swear I will" I turned around to see a female C.O. holding a can of mace pointed right at me. Aint this bout a bitch. What happen to the time when chicks wasn't even allowed to be C.O.s? Back in the days a nigga would have knocked her out and locked the bitch in a broom closet, but I guess things changed. She cuffed me as other officers ran in the unit and took homeboy to the hospital. I bet he aint gonna do no shit like that again. They took me to the S.H.U., special housing unit, the hole, whatever you want to call it. All I know is the cell was dark and cold.

There was nothing in there but an iron bed and a mattress, no light, no pillow, no books, no nothing. For a fight they usually leave you in there for thirty days but I hit that pussy nigga with the phone. I'm definitely looking at six months in here easy.

I started to make my bed. I was under a great amount of stress and figured I'd try to sleep it off. 'Where did I go wrong' I asked myself. I had a good team, I made sure everybody was eating; nobody was hungry—nobody! Everybody got houses, clothes, jewelry and would never have to worry about a god damn thing again as long as they lived and these un-loyal bitches left me to face this by myself.

"A yo! What up homie?" I snapped out of my thoughts and looked up to see the porter at my cell. In the hole we're locked in for 23 hours of the day. With that other hour you can go to rec or get a shower, but the porter was out all day giving out toilette paper, envelopes, writing paper, or passing shit to a nigga in another cell for you. Most of the porters get tired of doing shit for you and become straight dick heads.

"What's good my nigga?" I said walking up to the cell door. I noticed dude was on his tippy toes. He was so short he couldn't see over the little window that looked in your cell without a boost.

"Aint shit, where you from blood?"

"I'm from the Bronx, but I aint blood you heard."

"Oh so what you crip?" dude asked, his whole facial expression changing. He got more cold and ready to get at me the first chance he got.

"Nah I'm neutral ya dig."

"Oh okay, what you in the hole for blood?" I could tell dude was burned out on his blood shit, he probably been banging his whole life and all he knows is this blood shit.

"I popped on some nigga over the phone."

"Oh yeah, I heard about that. Word travels fast around here. That's some brave shit you did blood. That was that lil' nigga lil' Dee. I told that nigga somebody was gonna call his bluff one day. Anyway, they call me lil' Bad Azz, who you?"

"Thugga" lil Bad Azz was at least 5 foot 2, light skinned with a slim but muscular frame. By the look at the scars on his face and knuckles it looked like he loved to fight, might even have that Napoleon complex. You know, 'yeah im little but I will fuck you up' type shit.

"Okay Thugga get your shit together and if you need anything just holla at me you heard."

"Aight" I watched as lil' Bad Azz walked away. Just the look in his face, his bop and swagger told me the lil nigga was a force to be reckoned with. I laid my head on the bed I must have been tired from the last few days of events because before you know it I was out. I woke up a few hours later to hear lil' Bad Azz screaming at a nigga.

"Shut the fuck up pussy, this a blood jail, crips don't live here."

"I jumped off the bed to see what was going on and seen Bad Azz in front of cell number 7 with two cups in his hand and tossed one on the kid in the cell. I been to jail before so I already knew what that was, Piss. Niggas be pissing in cups and letting it sit for months that way its extra stink. A nigga will shit in a cup and do the same thing. There aint no showers until tomorrow so I knew dude was mad. Then I seen Bad Azz toss the other cup, "now sleep in that crab" Bad Azz had threw the other cup on duke bed, now he had to sleep on the floor, or the metal that was under the mattress, I had to laugh. Bad Azz must have heard me because he turned back and tossed up a gang sign.

"Yeah blood this how we do, fuck wrong with this crip nigga? He thought he was gonna live down here?" Bad Azz turned back to the crip nigga, "nigga imma shit and piss you down every day as long as you down here with me nigga!"

"What's going on in there?" an officer yelled.

"Nothing. Why, what's up?"

"It's lock in time Bad Azz." Shit, he must have been down here for a while cause even the C.O.'s called him Bad Azz.

"Aight." I seen Bad Azz lock himself in cell ten. I made a mental note to remember just in case this fool tried to play me and I ever get a chance to make it down to his cell, I'd fuck his little ass up. The C.O. finally cut the lights in the cell on and I got a chance to see what my cell really looked like. Shit was fucked up in here. The tile on the floor was chipped up, there was rat shit on the floor and writings all over the walls. I decided to read some, 'Blood up! Killer was here', 'money over bitches', 'hoe's aint shit', 'for a good time call Simone 555-395-0777', 'Alex is a rat' and finally 'lil Bad Azz Brooklyn don'. So bad azz was from B.K. huh!

"A yo! Thugga!"

"Who dat?"

"Never who dat, dis Bad Azz tho. Yo! Make yourself a line I got something for you."

"Aight." I looked around my cell for something I could use for some string. When I couldn't find anything I ripped off the thin end of my sheets. I looked around to find something else with a little weight to it. I finally spotted a mustache comb. The jail gives it to you to comb your hair with it. I tightened the sheet to it, that's what they call a line. I looked out the window of my cell to get a clear look at Bad Azz cell and slide the comb across the floor sliding it right in bad azz cell. That's what they call fishing.

"Aight pull it back in." I pulled the line back in and Bad Azz had tied the comb and string around an envelope. I opened it and there was a note inside.

*Yo homie I respect what you did in population. Not many niggas be poppin off now a days it's like the world is full with rats and bitch niggas so im sending you something to get your head right.*

I checked the envelope and Bad Azz had sent me some weed to smoke.

"Good looking sun."

"You already know."

Time was flying in the hole. I got used to how shit run down here, but I still couldn't wait to get the fuck up out this nasty mother fucker. I don't get to use the phone down this bitch, but Baby Blue comes to see me every day. At least I get to see my baby girl and rub her stomach.

My lawyer be coming to see me, so he working hard on my case. He hired a private investigator; he said he's determined to beat this shit. I'm happy I got a lawyer who's gonna fight for my freedom. A lot of these fucking lawyers take your money and don't give your case the attention it deserves.

Over the last few months me and Bad Azz got close. He still be setting me out with weed, and that's a good look, at least I get my head right when I'm stressed. He also got me a porter job so me and him be on the tier buggin out, high as shit, bidding off some of these fools. But we mostly bid off this crip nigga. Bad Azz does whatever he wants to that nigga. Spit in is food,

174

put boogers in it, he even spreaded shit on the nigga baked chicken. He buggin tho. If son don't eat soon he gonna die on niggas and we fuck around and have a brand new murder charge.

"Yo! Thugga I need some hot water sun, I got a visit today."

"I got you kid." That's my nigga Stone. I fucks with him, sun a good nigga. He from the Bronx too, Allerton Ave.

"Yo homie, can you help a nigga out dog, I need some hot water too."

"Hell nah, yo Thugga who dat? That crip nigga?"

"Yeah B.A."

"Oh man, soft ass nigga you thought my homeboy was gonna help you out? You got life fucked up" Bad Azz spit on the crip nigga and I laughed so hard I almost pissed on myself.

"Bad Azz, Thugga, lock in we got a new guy coming in."

"Aight we got you." I told the C.O. it was standard for them to lock us in whenever someone new comes in so just in case one of us had beef with him we couldn't beat him up

175

while he was in handcuffs. We locked in and I went to my mattress and got my eye spy that I had hid. The C.O.s didn't want us to have it because we could see what was going on, on the tier when we weren't suppose to. The eye spy is just a broken peace of mirror held together on a spoon by some toothpaste. I stuck the eye spy out my cell and couldn't believe what I was looking at. I seen this pussy ass midget mother fucker lil' Dee cuffed up coming down the tier. I pulled the eye spy back before the C.O. got a chance to see it. Lil' Dee walked by my cell but didn't see me.

"Oh shit, look what we got here, that scar held up real nice homie, real nice" I said as lil' Dee looked up to see the smile on my face. I ran in back of my cell to get my bag of shit I was saving for the crip nigga, but now had lil' Dee's name all over it. Boy was this gonna be fun.

# Chapter 32

*Thugga six months later*

I'll never forget the first time Tina came to visit me in jail. The Rikers Island visiting holding area was dirty, loud and crowded. The C.O.s looked mean and intimidating while the faces of the visitors, mostly women and children, were sad and lonely. I spotted Tina as she spotted me, she smiled, walked over to me slowly, and gave me a hug instead of the kisses I usually get. I got a smile.

"What's wrong?"

"Everything Thugga, everything."

"Talk to me baby girl."

"Oh, you mean like you should have talked to me huh?"

"Man what you talking bout now shorty?"

"Well Thugga, it turns out Diamond has a friend who knew Ruby Red. Ruby told her she used to fuck you, Diamond told Kiki and Kiki killed Ruby."

"Shit." I said leaning back in my chair.

"Yeah shit huh! Why you think Kiki won't answer your calls? Tiff disappeared, Ruby's dead Kiki aint fucking with you, now all you got left is me."

"Shit! Kiki aint trippin off that."

"You got shit fucked up nigga. Kiki got with that female crew that work for Spider, the Y.G.B.s. They like Kiki, said she's a real type bitch, so now they deal with her. She get birds for the same price you did, then she took every project you use to sell to. You know how that go, every nigga love a big but and a smile so they all copping weight from her. She even put workers on Boston Rd. Yeah, all your blocks Thugga. Kiki has become the female you, you got nothing left, she took everything from you, everything."

I couldn't believe what I was hearing. Everything I had worked so hard for, killed for, and struggled for is gone. All of it, and the only person in the world I trusted has taken it from me, my Kiki. How could she be so heartless? After all I've done for her. Then I thought about all I've done to her, Karma's a bitch, and her name is Kiki.

"Okay look, what I need you to do is..." Tina cut me off.

"Nah nigga, do you remember how you treated me? And I needed you Thugga. You told me I would be okay fucking with you, you told me I wouldn't need for nothing and when the police raided my house it was Kiki who bailed me out. Kiki set me straight and made sure I got on my feet. Stupid nigga what makes you think it aint Kiki that got my loyalty? Look at your face Thugga, you look so fucking pathetic. Your gonna rot in here Thugga. You killed all your friends, your bitches don't want you no more, you're all alone nigga, and you'll die that way" Tina said getting up from the table.

"Were you going bitch?" I said getting up too "you can't do this to me, do you know who the fuck I am, I'm Thugga bitch—Thugga!" The C.O.s rushed me and grabbed my arms before I could grab Tina.

"You know what you sound like, some pathetic old nigga who use to have it and struggling to hold on to it. It's over and so are you." I couldn't believe what I was hearing. They think it's over for a nigga, like I'm dead or something, like my lawyer aint paid and their aint a chance I can get the fuck outta here. Tina looked back and I smiled as the C.O.s pulled me away. After the visit they degraded me. They told me to strip and spread my ass cheeks while a male officer looked in my ass and told me to lift my nuts and looked at my dick. I mean what type of nigga are you to sign up for a job where you look at dick, ass and balls all day. When your girl asks you what you do all day, what's your answer? 'Well I stared at a couple of assholes today, a big dick and some hairy balls?' This nigga aint nothing but a sucker in a uniform. He was probably scared to be a cop so I guess this will do. Anyway, I got back to my housing unit and jumped right on the phone, I needed help and I needed someone by my side I needed Tiffany.

# Chapter 33

*Tiffany*

The last six months of my life have been wonderful. After I left Thugga I moved to New Rochelle NY, about 20 minutes from the Bronx. I enrolled in school again where I met the man of my dreams. We met passing in the school's hallway one day and he introduced himself to me. He was real polite, well dressed as if he were on his way to a meeting rather than classes. He had a beautiful smile and was wearing what I believe was Gucci cologne for men, he smelled delicious.

He told me he was studying to be a lawyer. 'Nice profession, my mother would love him' I thought, lawyers do very well in life and go far. As we walked through the hallways and I listened to him, he asked me out to dinner later that night, and even though I wasn't sure if I was ready for dating again I accepted his offer, and I'm glad I did. Kevin was perfect for me, a well educated strong and powerful black brother. He graduated but stayed in school just to stay sharp. Over dinner that night I told him about me. My life, what I've been through and how I've changed. I lost my way, but I caught myself just in time before I fell.

He applauded me for going back to my old ways of being a classy woman and never letting a problem become an excuse. We've been inseparable for the last six months. He had shown me how a woman is supposed to be treated, and I love him for it.

"Tiffany" Kevin said as he walked through the door of our house.

"Hey honey you hungry? Dinner's ready."

"Tiff we gotta talk." When I seen the serious look on his face I was worried and went to the living room to sit down with him to see what was wrong.

"What is it Kevin, what's wrong?"

"Do you remember that case I told you about? The one where the client was accused of murdering his best friend and a Colombian in a drug deal gone wrong?"

"Yeah."

"You'll never believe who it is"

"Who?"

"Sean Clark."

My mouth dropped, "honey are you sure?"

"Yeah, he called me today and asked me if I can locate someone and ask her to come and see him, when I asked who he said Tiffany Jones. I asked what the relation was and he said his ex-girlfriend."

"Oh God honey. Well what are you going to do?"

"Well Tiffany that's what I wanted to talk to you about, I thought about dropping the case because of the conflict of interest."

"Well there you have it."

"But let's be reasonable Tiff, I took an oath in law school."

"To do what, defend low life women beating murderers?"

"Now Tiff we don't know if he killed that man. He's capable, but did he?"

"Kevin!"

"Look Tiffany I hate it just as much as you do, but I just graduated law school, this case can be good for me."

"Kevin—he used to beat me!"

"That's not what he's on trial for Tiffany, let God be the judge for that."

# Chapter 34

*The Celebration*

When I found out Dollar had set up Black I told Kiki first, that's when she told me the plan. Then I was supposed to let Thugga know, and he would go into a rage and kill all his workers. Then Kiki would finally work up the nerves to kill Thugga for all the pain he's caused her and then we could take over his multi-million dollar enterprise. But he got locked up before she could get to him. Six months later we're celebrating in Jamaica.

"Hey Tina I wish I coulda been there to see his face when you told him I aint have to kill him but still manage to take his life away" Kiki said.

"I wish you was there too"

"And what he said?" Diamond asked.

"Where you going bitch? You can't do this to me, do you know who I am? I'm Thugga bitch."

"You're terrible" I said as we all laughed.

"Nah Chrystal you just had to see it, it was sad."

185

"I know it was" I told Tina as I looked around at Diamond and Kiki and asked myself—'were we any better?' We're sitting here laughing at a man who's about to start trial and fight for his life, does that make us haters? Man what am I doing worried about some nigga I wasn't fucking when we're sitting on a beach in Jamaica called Dunns River Falls. Yesterday we went to swim with the dolphins at Dolphins Cove. I had so much fun, I'm glad I got with Kiki and them but she was changing. I had to watch her, it look like she was letting the money and power get to her head. We went to a beach party, Guinness party, and a club named Asylum over in Kingston, we was all over that island. It was my very first sound clash—that shit was hot, it's were two different D.J.s play music and the crowd cheers for who they think is the best. That's when I caught Kiki watching me. She's been doing it ever since we left the hospital from seeing Black; oh yeah, he's doing well too. They say they expect him to make it. The doctor says he moves his right index finger whenever someone's in the room, which is a good thing.  I can't wait until he fully recovers.

"Damn Chrystal what you thinking about?" There she was watching me again, what's good with this bitch?

"I was wondering where we were going tonight."

"Oh that's easy, there's this popular club in Ocho Rios called Margaritaville. Me and Thugga been there before, ya'll gonna love it, drinks, food, and dancing. Matter a fact we should go and get ready, four bitches getting dressed, do you know how long that's gonna take?"

We jumped out of the rental in front of the club. The Jamaican night air felt so good on my skin. I was wearing a Fendi dress with the back out and Kiki was wearing a Gucci cat suit. Both Diamond and Tina were wearing shorts so short I thought their pussies would pop out any second now. But shit we were doing the damn thing tonight, we was the best thing moving up in this bitch. Every nigga we walked by tried to holla, I just couldn't understand the accents. We got a lot of Jamaican niggas in the Bronx but these niggas over here was even harder to understand. That didn't stop us from dancing the night away with these sexy island men though, and drinking every tropical drink on the island. After about an hour of dancing we got a table and decided to order some food, this would be my first Jamaican dish ever. I ordered the jerk chicken, bread fruit and a carrot juice to drink, and enjoyed every bit of it.

They played an old Buju Bonton slow song I knew. "Oh this is my jam" Kiki said, "I'm tired of these thirsty mother fuckers, come on Chrystal let's dance." "Okay" me and Kiki hit the floor with the intention of making every man in this place jealous, and boy was it working. I looked over at Diamond and Tina when Kiki took me by my hand and spun me; she pulled me towards her and positioned my back against her breast. She started to rub my thighs and caressing my breast, it felt good and I didn't want her to stop.

"I heard you gave Black a threesome" Kiki whispered in my ear so softly it gave me a chill.

"Yeah I fuck with him like that."

"That would mean you're into girls."

"I can appreciate the female body."

"Me too."

The next thing I know we're in the hotel—wet pussy everywhere. Me and Kiki soaked the sheets, and I loved every minute of it. I never tasted a pussy so sweet, I could see why Kiki had niggas open. She laid me down and sucked on my clit like it was strawberry flavored. As she wiggled her tongue over it she made eye contact with me; that turned me on. She put two fingers in me and sucked my pussy lips. My pussy was so wet I could hear noises as her fingers went in and out of my pussy. I wish I knew she got down like this, I would have brought the strap-on and told her to fuck me from the back, I wanted to explode all in her mouth but I held back. It felt too good to let it end now.

"You like the way I suck this pussy Chrystal?"

"Yes!"

"I've been watching your sexy ass for a long time, I knew you tasted this good."

"You like it Kiki?"

"Yes!"

"Then suck it baby, suck it till I come all over your lips, face, and tongue. Ahhh, yeah, yeah bitch, right there, right there, don't stop baby, yessss! Put the fingers back in me bitch just like that, yeah, yeah, yeah yeaaah!"

Visit omygahshproductions.com

For music, flyers, book covers, and more.

# Chapter 35

*Kevin*

I went to see my client today; there was so much to talk about. I had to figure a way to get him off the hook. If I beat this case it would be good for my career. People would start to notice me, and I might even make partner, or start my own firm because of it. I was looking for a way to tell Sean that Tiffany was my woman, and that we were in love. I'm a man in every sense of the word, it's not that I'm afraid to tell him, it's just that in his predicament he needs someone and I was about to tell him the only person he could count on won't be there for him. I walked pass the prison security and signed the log in book that kept track of who visited the inmates. I was escorted to a private room that was for attorney and client visits only. I pulled out Sean's file with all the information on the case I received from the prosecutor and patiently waited on his arrival. They brought him in and un-cuffed him, I watched as he took a seat in front of me and leaned back. It's been a week since I seen him but prison changes people fast. I guess you have to change, become meaner, colder, and tougher. In jail only the strong survive and everyone else gets run over, stepped on, extorted and whatever else you could imagine.

"How you doing Sean?"

"How do I look Kevin?"

"Come on now, I didn't put you here Sean."

"And you aint doing shit to get me out either."

"That was the judge's decision not mine."

"You got good news for me or what?"

"Few questions first, but yes some good news."

"Sure go head."

"You going to trial?"

"Let me see, life or the death penalty, hmmmm! Let me see which one should I choose?"

"I guess that means you're going to trial, look I spoke to the prosecutor about the gun case, your co-defendant Tina Williams copped out to probation. She had no priors so she didn't face jail time, but they're offering you five years, you want to take it or you want to go to trial on that too?"

"I'll take the five I can deal with that."

"Okay, for the murder and attempt murder I asked for a speedy trial which means they have thirty days to take us to trial and it doesn't really give them enough time to collect any more evidence."

"I was thinking Kevin...if Black"—

"I was getting to that. I spoke to the prosecutor this morning, it turns out Black had a gun on him that had Paco's finger prints on it. The way their looking at it Black killed Paco in self defense and took his gun, they're gonna give Black a gun charge. He has no priors either so if he wakes out of his coma he'll get probation just like Tina. So they dropped the murder charge on you, all you have is the attempted murder."

"And how much time does that carry?"

"Well it still carries life but at least we only have one charge to beat instead of two."

"Did you find Tiffany Jones?"

"Yeah I did Sean."

"Word!? What the bitch say?"

"Must we call her a bitch?"

"Man what the fuck you care?"

"Because Sean", I leaned over the table, "she belongs to me now."

# Chapter 36

*Diamond and Kiki*

Kiki had a big delivery that she was kind of worried about. This nigga orders five birds a week and all of a sudden he wants fifty birds so she wants all of us to park on different parts of the block in tinted out whips. He's suppose to hand her cash and once she checks it out she'll give him the car keys to the hoopty with the birds in the trunk. So I drove over to Edenwald projects and watched this nigga Bird for about an hour. It all looked good so I hit Kiki on the chirp.

"Chirp! Yo! Shit looking good on this end"

"Chirp! Aight I'm on my way, be there in like two minutes" I tossed the phone down, cocked the mac I had in my lap and sparked my blunt. I aint smoke all day and right now felt like a good time. I let the window down on my side to let the smoke out, that's when I heard someone across the street on the phone.

"Yeah she's on her way, look as soon as I get the coke I'll be there." That must be Bird I thought to myself, this nigga is mad reckless. Talking on the phone like that, that's how crews go down. If the police was listening we would all be on the same indictment. Small time hustling ass nigga, fuck wrong with him. Just then I seen Kiki pulling up and I chirped the other girls.

"Chirp! Yo! Everyone on point we got action."

"I see her" Tina hit me back and Chrystal was in the car in front of me so I knew she was on point.

I turned into Edenwald, I parked my car and looked up at Bird, he was smiling at me, that shit sent chills through my spine. I had a bad feeling about this deal so I had all my girls out here on point. I mean shit, if it was gonna go down we were gonna have the upper hand. What Bird didn't know was Diamond, Tina and Chrystal were parked on his block, all with automatic weapons, and they were ready to put on in his head if he thought shit was sweet because I was a chick.

"Bird what up?"

"I'm good baby girl how you?"

"I'm living and that's all I can ask for now a days I guess."

"Okay, okay, how's Thugga?"

"He chillin."

"That's not what I heard, the streets got it that he's locked up."

"Look, we doing business or what?"

"Sure where the work at?"

"Where's my fucking money nigga?"

"Right here in this bag" Bird raised a bag I didn't know he was carrying, I'm fucking slipping. As he lowered the bag I noticed a nigga looking out the projects window with something in his hands.

"Oh shit" by the time I turned around to run I noticed Diamond, Tina and Crystal jumping out their cars, they must have spotted him the same time I did.

"Pop, pop, pop."

"Boom! Boom! Boom!"

"Clap, clap, clap"

That stunt Bird pulled cost us our friend, Tina got hit in her chest. We rushed her to the hospital but her lungs already collapsed...it was too late. I got a mystery call from a nigga who caught Bird that night, stabbed him to death and hung him on a pole in the projects as a message to everyone not to fuck with us. For that, he wants to be a partner, and we gladly let him in. If you let him tell it he's been watching us for a while and will continue to and will enforce whenever necessary.

# Chapter 37

We were at the end of my trial and the prosecutor was pulling out all the stunts but Kevin was eating him up like a lion on a rabbit. And I was enjoying every minute of it. I had on a navy blue suit, pocket square with matching tie, cufflinks and my waves on spin. Shit I even caught some of the bitches in the jury watching me every now and then, which was a good look for me. If I beat this all I gotta do is five years up north for a gun charge. I had to beat this. I got a visit from Baby Blue yesterday, Kiki went to cop weight from them and told them I was on the island. She also told her Tina got killed in a drop off that went wrong. I felt like shorty did me wrong when I needed her but I was sorry she died, I aint want nothing like that to happen to her. But I did get some good news. The night that Baby Blue and me got it in she got pregnant. Yep, a nigga got a second chance at being a father again.

"I rest my case your honor."

"Okay thank you, Mr. Allen your closing argument please."

"Thank you. Ladies and gentlemen of the jury, you have heard it all today. The story of three men, one shot and killed, the other in a coma and then theirs my client. His finger prints, his frequent visits, his friendship to the deceased but I ask you ladies and gentlemen, if you have a friend that neighbors say frequently visits you wouldn't he leave fingerprints in your house?...... He visits often, he could be a business partner, a babysitter, maybe even a gay lover" Kevin told the jury. "In order to convict a man of murder the law says you should have no reasonable doubts he committed these crimes, ladies and gentlemen of the jury—any doubts? Your honor, I rest my case."

"Okay, court will adjourn until the jury reaches their decision."

"Yo! Kevin come talk to me while the jury's out, I got a few things I wanna holla at you about." The jury went in one room to vote while the marshal took me in the back room to wait for their decision. I was nervous as fuck dog. I smiled when I seen Kevin walk through the door.

"Good job Kevin I gotta give it to you, it was a job well done."

"Thank you sir." Kevin said taking a bow like an actor who just finished a good performance. "I got a good feeling about this Sean, real good feeling."

"Me too Kevin, the prosecutor fucked up. I mean sure my fingerprints are there but if no one can say I was there that night and they saying that Black killed Paco in self defense, then shit aint it hard to believe I tried to kill a boy I raised?"

"You sure right about that Sean" the silence in the room was awkward.

"How's Tiffany Kevin?"

"She's okay."

"She never talked about me?"

"No, we talk about us."

"She ever tell you I'm the one that showed her how to swallow?"

"Were not gonna do this Sean."

"I used to make her scream Kevin, twist her body in every position possible."

"Shut up!"

"She's just like me Kevin, she steals, robs kills."

"Shut up!"

"The next time you fuck her just know she use to moan like that for me too."

"Shut the fuck up!" Kevin lost control banged his fist on the table in front of us and stood up, I jumped up too and was ready to fuck him up when a guard walked in.

"Mr. Clark. Mr. Allen the jury has reached their decision."

"Order in the court", the judge announced.

"Has the jury reached their decision?" he asked.

"Yes your honor."

"You may read it" a slim black lady stood and opened up the folded piece of paper.

"We the jury find Sean Clark...innocent of attempt murder."

# Chapter 38

*Thugga*

Oh! It was on and poppin now. It's been a few months since I beat my trial and all I could think about was hitting the streets, word up! I know I have four years left but that aint nothing, I could do that standing on my head. The streets was all that I was thinking about as I was in my cell adding water to the little bit of shampoo I had just poured in to a water bottle. I locked the bottle and shook it up, looked at my cell door to make sure the C.O. wasn't around then drank it. No sooner then I swallowed, I threw up in my sink, nothing! I drank some more and this time I pushed out two red balloons. I hate throwing up but shit, this is the only way I was gonna get the drugs in that Baby Blue brought me once a week.

That's my ride or die chick for real. She sends me money whenever I need it without me having to ask, she never misses my visits and one day, when my visit was over I leaned in for a kiss and she slipped something from her mouth to mine. I instantly knew what it was, and she been bring me weed ever since. My baby also had been keeping me up on what's been going on in the streets. I knew all about how good Kiki was doing, the fact that she moved Crystal into her house and they got this little lesbian love thing going on—they make me sick. I'm hearing Diamond was making a real name for herself out there in the streets. She's putting nothing but work in, and got zero tolerance for certain shit. Niggas and bitches alike is falling in love with her; I aint mad at her baby do your thing, but she aint a match for my Baby Blue.

I wiped the balloons off, cleaned out my sink and rolled me a blunt lying down on my bed. As I smoked I was good because the C.O.s did they count and wouldn't be coming back around for another two hours. I had pictures of Baby Blue on the wall; I smiled when I looked at her. She sent me pictures in thongs and shit before her stomach started to show, shorty is truly sexy as shit. I smoked the rest of the blunt and flushed the roach down the toilette falling asleep with her on my mind.

"Mr. Clark—Mr. Clark!" the C.O. woke me out of my sleep, "wake up your on the pack out, take all your personal belongings and leave the rest." I checked the time...2:00 am.

"Where am I going?"

"Up north, they'll tell you what jail when you get to R and D."

"Aight." Shit it was about that time. I couldn't wait to get off the island. Up north had more freedom. You could stay outside longer, they had longer visits and time flew a lil' faster. I packed everything I knew I could bring with me, my baby mother's pictures and letters, that was it, niggas had to leave their clothes and food. But my account was full so who really gives a fuck. Now up north is where niggas be getting it poppin at so as I waited I prepared my mind. 'Well Thugga' I said to myself 'this is it, you know how it go it's kill or be killed, just get up that bitch, get a knife, and bring it to any nigga who look at you wrong.'

"Clark you ready?"

"Yeah." They brought me down to R and D, took my personal property and put it in a box with my name and numbers on it. They put it on the bus so it will get there with me. Then put me in a cell of 50 niggas going to my jail. They stripped searched me again and cuffed my hand and feet and at about ten a.m. we rolled out. I was mad as shit, what was the fucking reason for them to wake us up at two in the morning if we wasn't gonna leave for another eight hours. We finally pulled up in front of the jail eight p.m. that night that's when I seen the sign that said Greene Correctional Facility.

I looked out the bus window and noticed four C.O.s with guns. There was one in front of the bus standing beside a truck with a shot gun in his hand, another behind the bus with an automatic weapon and one by the R and D that appeared to be a glock. That's when I seen a fat white C.O. walk on the bus.

"Ok listen up gentlemen, you're not in Kansas anymore, this is Greene Correctional Facility. Here we have zero tolerance for stupidity, for violence, and for gang activity. If you partake in any of the three we will send you to a jail so far your family will never see you. Do you understand me? Ok, when I call your name come to the front and give me your ID number" as I listen to this cracker call names I thought about Baby Blue and my child. I wondered if it would be a boy or girl, not that it mattered, I would love the baby with all my heart no matter what.

"Sean Clark", I got up and walked towards him.

"97R4816"

"Good, walk down to that officer down their boy." Boy! I can't believe this, this cracker that would never look me in the face on the street just called me a boy. They took five of us at a time into a changing room and stripped us out again. I couldn't believe it, a C.O. must be a gay man's dream job, all they do is look at assholes all day.

"Okay gentlemen, look at that desk you'll find your name I.D. card and housing unit you're going to."

KITTY KAT CREW

A Novel by B.R.

Coming soon

# Chapter 39

"A yo homie, you can't sit here."

"What the fuck you mean I can't sit here?"

"This a Brooklyn table, the word on the pound has it you from the Bronx."

"Okay so what of it?" I asked getting up from the mess hall table. I was about to rock this nigga jaw when out of no were some nigga knocked him out for me.

"Yo! Come on let's get out of here before the C.O. see what's going on. Come on nigga" I followed dude from the mess hall to the yard.

"A yo son what your name is?"

"Thugga"

"Aight Thugga, I'm Rome."

"Okay, okay good looking Rome but you don't even know me, why you help me back there?"

"Come on spin the track with me." Rome handed me a cigarette and we smoked while we walked around the yard. "I helped you because

I heard you from the Bronx, it's only a handful of us down here so we gotta stick together. The majority on this pound is Brooklyn niggas."

"So basically we just started a Bronx Brooklyn beef then."

"Nah, they shot caller gonna come holla at me later. I stay bringing it to them niggas hard, they don't really want it with me dog, and my knife game is silly. Which reminds me, I brought you out a razor and a knife which one you want?"

"Both" Rome looked at me and took a pull of his cigarette.

"Good man. Look like I finally got me a rida up here with me huh!?"

"Shit, you already know"

"What unit you in Thugga?"

"3B"

"Okay I'm in 3A. You need anything from me just holla." Rome handed me a street razor and a knife made out of fiberglass with black tape at the end. I looked around to make sure nobody seen him hand it to me and stuck them both in my pocket.

"Good looking doggy, what part of the Bronx you from anyway?"

"Tracy Towers, what about you?"

"Boston Rd."

"Oh okay, I use to fuck with this bitch up there name Chrystal, you know her?"

"Yeah I know that bitch, she a jump off tho my nigga."

"Yeah I know, but don't you just love a jump off? You aint never got to tell them what to do, they already know, suck dick, balls, take it in the ass and leave the crib before your girl get home." Me and Rome laughed, I could fuck with this nigga he just like me. He looked to be about 21, he was shorter then I was in muscle mass, but it was only right he been up hear lifting weights while I was on the island. All you could do was pull-ups push-ups and dips.

"Yard recall" the officer yelled over the loud speaker.

"Yo! Their aint no more movement for the day dog I'll get with you in the morning, and Thugga be on point this aint no sweet spot, shit be poppin up here."

"I can dig it."

Get Right

A Novel by B.R.

Coming Soon

# Chapter 40

*Thugga*

Over the years me and Rome became cool. He's a good nigga and he goes hard. No matter what I wanted to do he's down for it, so we ran around the compound and gave niggas hell. Extorting niggas, beating up snitches, and showing Brooklyn niggas that Bronx niggas get it in too. Me and Rome had about twenty fights a piece since I been here, and aint lose one. It helped the time pass.

As for me and Baby Blue, we doing good. My lil' mama had a boy, Sean Clark Jr. My lil' man getting big too, he started walking and he talks a little bit. He says Daddy real clear, that makes me smile every time I hear it. I even asked Baby Blue to marry me, of course she said yes, so as soon as I leave here that's the first thing we're gonna do. But right now I had something to take care of.

Me and Rome hit the yard, it turns out that the nigga from the Bronx I fucked up on the Island over the phone named lil' Dee just got here last night. Another nigga named Red from the

Bronx brought him to the gym to meet all the Bronx niggas, when me and lil' Dee locked eyes I thought we were gonna start banging right then and there. We exchanged words before niggas broke it up. But today I was gonna punish his bitch ass worst than I did the first time.

"Damn what you gonna do when you get home my nigga?"

"What you mean what imma do when I get home? Imma take over."

"What about Kiki?"

"What about that bitch?"

"The streets say she got it my nigga, she running shit in the hood my nigga."

"Don't worry about Kiki." I said as me and Rome spun the track in the yard, I lit cigarette and took a good look at Rome. Sun's a good nigga, he been holding me down ever since I hit the pound. "Yo sun what year you come home my nigga?"

"2015 I got five years left on my bid."

"Drug case right.?"

"Yeah why?"

"Just thinking my nigga. If you get home and all your plan's fail, come fuck with me imma make sure you good."

"Yeah you already know." Right then I noticed that nigga lil' Dee and his homie Red coming and I seen Rome get on point.

"Yo! Thugga what's all that shit you was poppin in the gym last night nigga?" before I could answer Rome snuffed the nigga Red in his nose and I pulled out my razor and ate the nigga lil' Dee. I cut the nigga from the top of his head to his chin something terrible. Blood flew all over Red and Rome. I tossed the razor and told Rome lets bounce but the fucking Rec. officer seen what happen and press the read button on his radio alerting every C.O. in the jail some kind of violence poppin off. I heard one warning shot from the gun tower and the C.O. yell.

"Everybody on the ground NOW!" We all knew what that meant. When that warning shot go off, if you aint hit the ground, the next shot was going in the crowd full of inmates. As I looked around every nigga that came to the yard was eating grass, no one wanted to be the one who got shot with those rubber bullets. The C.O.s shot these hard ass rubber bullets out of some assault rifles. I watched as the C.O.'s ran in our direction and grabbed lil'

Dee's punk ass off the ground. They was probably gonna take him to an outside hospital to get his bitch ass stitched up.

"This aint over Thugga." Lil' Dee said, still gushing blood from his face.

"Where the fuck they do that at? Since when we start dry snitching?" I couldn't believe lil' Dee just said that shit. They cuffed me, Rome, and Red then took us to the hole.

We only stayed in the hole a week. The C.O. didn't actually see who did the cutting. They just knew we were around. And lil' Dee didn't out right snitch when they asked so the warden had no choice but to let me Rome and Red out. They shipped lil' Dee out because they didn't know who he had beef with, and if it's over or not. We let red live because Rome popped first, he aint wait to see how Red was gonna react. Seeing that Red just met lil' Dee the day before, we don't think he was holding him down. Red just aint too bright, and didn't know how serious shit was. But everything is back to normal now. They put me and Rome in the same unit which was cool, his cell was a few doors down from mine. I don't know if they thought that was a good idea putting us together, but they were wrong. The first thing I did was give Rome my baby mother information so we wouldn't lose contact. I gave him lil' Bad Azz shit too, seeing how they come home around the same time. Rome gave me his sister and brother information. With that said we started to do what gangstas do.

"Yo Rome, lemme holla at you in my sell real fast kid."

" Yeah whats poppin Thugga?" Rome asked as he stepped in my cell.

"Yo, whats good with fam in that cell over their?" I pointed to the cell in front of mine.

"That's Tony, he a good nigga. He from Atlanta, why what up?"

"Nah, that nigga came back from a visit bout an hour ago and he still got that mother fuckin curtain up. Shit, where I come from nigga, he shittin them drugs out." See not everyone in jail swallowed their drugs the way I did. Some niggas was afraid the bag would pop in their stomach and then they gotta get rushed to the hospital. If the doctor had to pump it out, the C.O.s would get it and charge you for the shit. So some niggas grease up they ass hole with whatever they got, lotion, Vaseline, hair grease, butter, whatever and stick the drugs up they asshole and shit it back out after the visit.

"Oh word then what the fuck we waiting on nigga?" Rome asked as we headed for Tony's cell. Rome swung the door open and I ran down on this fool.

"Yo! What's poppin young nigga? Oh man Rome look what we got here" sure enough this ATL ass nigga was washing off at least five balloons in his sink. Some of it still had shit on it. I can tell you one thing dude needs an autopsy cause it smelled like someone died up in him.

"Okay, okay I see we on point huh Tony." Rome said closing the door behind him and pulling his T-shirt over his nose to because of the smell.

"A shawty, what the fuck yall doin' bruh?"

"Shut the fuck up!" I said smacking the shit out of Tony's punk ass. He covered his face like he expected another one to come.

"Chill shawty, yo Rome, tell your homie to chill you know I don't want no problem folk."

"Why the fuck you aint tell me you was getting drug's fool?" Rome said grabbing dude shirt collar up. "You mean all this time you was straight and wasn't braking me off?" Rome tossed dude to the floor stomping him with his tim's as dude curled up like a new born.

"Yo! Check this out" I told him "from now on, whatever you get on that visit floor, me and Rome want half of it, hear me!?"

"I got ya'll boys" Tony answered still rolled up on the floor.

"For now tho we gonna start with this." Rome turned on the hot water in the sink, washed off the rest of the shit that was left on the balloon, dried them off with a towel hanging on the wall then stuffed them in his pocket as we walked out Tony's cell leaving him in his cell still on the floor curled up. We went back to my cell putting up a towel to block the view from anyone seeing inside. The C.O. wouldn't fuck with it cause niggas put towels up when they shitting, and that's what they would think im doing. Rome sat at my desk in my cell and popped all five of the balloons open. Four of them had weed and one had dope.

"Thugga, I already know what you thinking but imma take one of these weed bags and smoke. Here, sell the rest big homie." He threw me the rest of them.

"You already know, we'll split the profit down the middle." This was perfect, now I could smoke the shit my baby mom bring me and get money off Tony shit.

"Chow time fellas, get ready for lunch." I heard the C.O. yell.

"I'll be back my nigga lemme get dressed. Don't leave me kid." Rome went to get dressed for chow, I did the same. I took my Tims and Russell sweat pants off and put on my state greens and black state boots on. It was mandatory to put it on in the day time if you were leaving the unit. I stashed the drugs under my sink in the cell and rolled out.

"Rome hurry the fuck up doggy!"

"Here I go, I just wanted to get my knife just in case these ATL niggas start feeling themselves."

"Please nigga, aint but three of them pussy niggas on the pound, come on we out."

We hit the walk way saying what up to the nigga's we fuck with, a few were happy we were out the hole while others had fear in their eyes. We got on line for the food, I got my tray and wasn't surprised that the meatloaf looked like dog food. Everything they served in here was some shit except for chicken day and McDonald day. On chicken day we get fried chicken, on Wednesdays they serve burgers and fries so niggas called it McDonald day, best day of the week if you ask me. We sat at the Bronx table right next to the Brooklyn table.

Now I got weed and that boy for sale—boy means dope. I went to the Brooklyn and let them know. Everybody said they would holla at me tonight in the gym so me and Rome went back to the cell to bag up.

I took a razor and chopped the weed up as fine as I could, sticks, seeds and all to make the shit appear bigger than it was. Then I slid it to Rome to bag up, not in bags but in what we called papers. Rome would tear a small piece of writing paper and dump a small amount of weed in it, so small that if a nigga tried to sell it to you on the street you would probably smack the shit out of him. I mean it was like the dust you would sweep up off a clean floor the shit wasn't even worth a dollar on the streets, but you gotta remember, our system is so clean in jail we could get high off anything so Rome folded the shit up and since there's no tape in jail he used the label off the deodorant. It worked the same, and that's a paper. We did the same with the dope, but just enough for one hit and then we hit the gym. We brought Tony with us. We held the drugs but I wanted Tony to hold the money so the C.O.s wouldn't find both on me if they became suspicious of my movements. I should have been got this nigga. We sold so much drugs that night Tony had to go back and forth from the gym to the unit just to drop money off in my cell. Money in jail is cigarettes. No matter what you wanted to buy, weed, dope, food out the kitchen, knives, razors, whatever, you had to use cigarettes. We charge five packs of cigarettes for one paper of weed and ten packs for a paper of boy.

"Shit we got something here Thugga. Too bad you about to go home."

"Hell yeah. Come on Rome, I'm a hustler. Put me anywhere on God's green earth, I'll triple my worth."

"Yeah aight, now you fucking Jay-z right." We laughed.

"Let's get out of here kid, it's almost lock in time. I'm tryna get right, then bust your ass in chess real fast."

"I hear that shit. You couldn't beat me in chess if you get right off this weed, boy, and had Tony here holding my hands nigga" we laughed. Rome's my nigga, I'm glad I met him.

# Chapter 41

*Kevin*

I was racing on my way home trying to get to the house before Tiffany got there. I was finally put in a position to own my own law firm and was gonna celebrate tonight. I've dreamed about this day forever and it finally came. I imagined the things me and Tiffany would do like finally stop renting a home and finally own one. I couldn't wait to take Tiffany shopping and buy her all the finest things that she loves so much. Imma take her on trips all around the world, I think we'll start with Africa, then maybe Rome, England, and other places in Europe. Where ever she wanted to go, as long as she's happy I wouldn't care. I took a look at the jewelry box on the car seat next to me. I had bought an engagement ring. I'm going to ask Tiffany to marry me, my life would be complete. Tiffany's my better half and I was ready to spend the rest of my life with her. I parked and got the flowers off the back seat of the car and a few groceries out the trunk. I figured I'd cook dinner instead of going out tonight. Eat over candle light, pop a bottle of champagne then pop the question.

I opened the door to my apartment heading straight for the kitchen to drop the groceries off, just then I noticed the house was darker than usual.

"Why are all the lights out?" when I turned the living room lights on I dropped the flowers on the floor. There was someone sitting on my couch. "Sean?"

"No one steals my girl Kevin."

# Chapter 42

"Hello."

"Hi honey, where are you?"

"I'm in the hair dresser."

"I love you so much!"

"I love you too Kevin what's going on?"

"A celebration, I got some good news to tell you."

"Really what is it?"

"I can't tell you yet, it will ruin my surprise"

"Okay, well I got some good news for you too!"

"What?"

"I can't tell you, it might ruin the surprise" I mimicked Kevin.

"Oh really funny, keep your little secret then, do you know what time you'll be home?"

"In about two hours."

"Perfect, I'm pulling up to the house now. And Tiffany, I love you."

"I love you too Kevin" I hung up the phone glowing. I know every woman has a man that's the best in their eyes but God has truly blessed me. Kevin is the most genuine generous, caring, sweetest, understanding man I've ever known in my life, and I love him with all my heart. As the hair dresser finished my hair I paid her, left the shop and jumped in the Lexus Kevin bought me for my birthday. As I started up the car and took off I couldn't wait to get home and tell Kevin the news, I'm two months pregnant. I was having his baby and felt on top of the world. I was also graduating college this year, life was going well and I deserved it. I parked my car and got in the elevator, reached my apartment and let myself in. "Kevin! Kevin baby I'm home! Where are you baby?" I walked in the kitchen and he wasn't there. He's so silly, it's just like him to hide and try to creep up behind me to surprise me, then start kissing me on my neck but not this time; this time it would be me to surprise him. I crept around the corner and into the living room, my knees went week instantly and I fell to the floor. Kevin laid their and there was blood everywhere. "No! no! Kevin no!" I crawled over to him then dialing 911.

"911, what's your emergency?"

"I need an ambulance my boyfriend has been shot in the head" I checked for a pulse but it was too late, there was none. As I looked down on him flashes of Jermaine went through my mind. My heart can't take this anymore.

# Chapter 43

I was sitting on the block with Diamond. Over the years me and her got closer, not on no lover shit just as friends. Chrystal was a little jealous but I assured her nothing was going on. I did let Chrystal know I had a man on the side though. I loved pussy but wasn't ready to give up no dick. She was cool with it. She said she understood so from time to time we would give him a threesome. I'm sure he thought he was coming up on two freak bitches but in all actuality we were just getting some dick whenever we needed it.

"Yo Diamond, that nigga Ghetto that be sweating you just drove by."

"Man fuck that nigga, he keep trying to floss his lil' money like I aint cakcd all the way the fuck up. He better stop playing before I rob his ass" we had a good laugh about that, but knowing Diamond she would really do that shit. She'd leave a nigga dead in his house fast over some bread.

"Yo! Lemme get the fuck outta here before he come back around. If you need me hit my jack tho!"

"I can dig it."

I'd been sitting across the street in a rental watching KiKi and Diamond for about an hour and couldn't wait for Diamond to leave so I could kill this bitch. I decided to spare Diamond, after all my beef aint with her. I'm pretty sure KiKi aint know I was home so I was about to catch her slippin. Fuck wrong with this bitch? She thought she was just gonna take everything from me and live on the same planet I was on? She got me fucked up. I got out the Buick I rented, her back was facing me so she aint even see me coming. I walked up on the curve and cocked the glock when she heard the sound it was too late, I had the drop on her.

"A yo Thugga." I spun around ready to clap whoever it was that called my name. My mouth flew open when I seen the desert eagle barrel pointed at me and the look of death in Black's eyes!

"Long time no see homeboy." Black pulled the trigger.

Look out for THUGGA Pt. 2

Coming soon.